The minute he slipped his arms around Anny to dance with her, the moment he felt her body fit itself to his, Demetrios knew he was done for.

He would have laughed bitterly at his own foolishness if the desire for her hadn't been so intense, if the longing hadn't been so real. Anger and desperation he could fight.

He couldn't fight this.

It was like having his dreams come true. It was like being offered a taste of all he'd ever longed for. A single spoonful that would have to last him for the rest of his life.

"To remember," Anny had said, as if it was a good thing.

How could it be good to have a hollow, aching reminder of the joy he'd once believed was his due? It wasn't. He didn't believe in promises anymore. Yet, as much as he tried not to give in, he couldn't resist.

It was like trying to resist gravity. Like agreeing to step off a cliff—then refusing to let himself fall.

Impossible.

All about the author...
Anne McAllister

RITA® Award-winner **ANNE McALLISTER** was born in California, spent formative summer vacations on the beach near her home and on her grandparents' small ranch in Colorado and visiting relatives in Montana. Studying the cowboys, the surfers and the beach volleyball players, she spent long hours developing her concept of "the perfect hero." (Have you noticed a lack of hard-driving type-A businessmen among them? Well, she promises to do one soon, just for a change!)

One thing she did do, early on, was develop a weakness for lean, dark-haired, handsome lone-wolf type guys. When she finally found one, he was in the university library where she was working. She knew a good man when she saw one. They've now been sharing "happily ever after" for over thirty years. They have four grown children, and a steadily increasing number of grandchildren. They also have three dogs who keep her fit by taking her on long walks every day.

Quite a few years ago they moved to the Midwest, but they spend more and more time in Montana. And as Anne says, she lives there in her head most of the time anyway. She wishes a small town like her very own Elmer, Montana, existed. She'd move there in a minute. But she loves visiting big cities as well, and New York has always been her favorite.

Before she started writing romances, Anne taught Spanish, capped deodorant bottles, copyedited textbooks, got a master's degree in theology and ghostwrote sermons. Strange and varied, perhaps, but all grist for the writer's mill, she says.

Anne McAllister

THE VIRGIN'S PROPOSITION

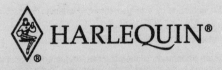

HARLEQUIN®

TORONTO • NEW YORK • LONDON
AMSTERDAM • PARIS • SYDNEY • HAMBURG
STOCKHOLM • ATHENS • TOKYO • MILAN • MADRID
PRAGUE • WARSAW • BUDAPEST • AUCKLAND

Recycling programs
for this product may
not exist in your area.

ISBN-13: 978-0-373-12944-7

THE VIRGIN'S PROPOSITION

First North American Publication 2010.

Copyright © 2010 by Anne McAllister.

THE VIRGIN'S
PROPOSITION

CHAPTER ONE

SOMEDAY HER PRINCE would come.

But apparently not anytime soon, Anny thought as she glanced down to check her watch discreetly once again.

She shifted in the upholstered armchair where she'd been waiting for the past forty minutes, then sat up even straighter, and craned her neck to look down the length of the Ritz-Carlton lobby for any sign of Gerard.

There were hundreds of other people milling about. In fact, the place was a madhouse.

It always was, of course, during Film Festival week in Cannes. The French seacoast town began overflowing with industry moguls, aspiring thespians, and avid filmgoers toward the end of the first week in May.

By now—three days into the festival—the normally serene elegant area near the hotel bar, where small genteel groups usually met for cocktails or apertifs, was now a sea of babbling people. The usual polite hushed voices of guests had been replaced by raucous cracks of masculine laughter and high-pitched flirty feminine giggles.

All around her, Anny heard rapid intense conversations rumbling and spiking as producers talked deals, directors flogged films, and journalists and photographers cornered the world's most sought-after actors and actresses. Everywhere she looked curious fans and onlookers, not to mention the hopeful groupies, milled about trying to look as if they belonged.

A prince would barely have been noticed.

But unless he was masquerading as a movie fan, which of course was ridiculous, there was no sign of tall distinguished Prince Gerard of Val de Comesque anywhere.

Anny was tempted to tap her impatient toes. She didn't. She smiled serenely instead.

"In public, you are serene, you are calm, you are happy," His Royal Highness, King Leopold Olivier Narcisse Bertrand of Mont Chamion—otherwise known as "Papa"—had drummed into her head from the cradle. "Always serene, my dear," he had repeated. "It is your duty."

Of course it was. Princesses were serene. And dutiful. And, of course, they were generally happy, too.

Privately Anny had always thought it would be the worst ingratitude if they weren't.

Being a princess certainly wasn't all fun and games as she knew from twenty-six years of personal experience. But princesses, by their mere birthright, were entitled to so much that none of them had a right to be anything but grateful.

So Her Royal Highness, Princess Adriana Anastasia Maria Christina Sophia of Mont Chamion, aka Anny, was serene, dutiful, determinedly happy. And grateful. Always.

Well, almost always.

At the moment, she was also stressed. She was impatient, annoyed and, if she were honest—with herself at least—a little bit apprehensive.

Not scared exactly. Certainly not panic-stricken.

Just vaguely sick to her stomach. Edgy. Filled with a sort of creeping dread that seemed to sneak up on her when she was least expecting it.

Except she had felt the dread so frequently over the past month that now she *was* expecting it. Regularly.

It was nerves, she told herself. Prewedding jitters. Never mind that the wedding was over a year away. Never mind that the date hadn't even been set yet. Never mind that Prince Gerard, sophisticated, handsome, elegant, and worldly, was everything a woman could ask for.

Except here.

She stood up so that she could scan the busy lobby once more. She'd had to dash to get to the hotel by five. Her father had called her this morning and said that Gerard would be expecting her, that he had something to discuss.

"But it's Thursday. I'll be at the clinic then," she had protested.

The clinic Alfonse de Jacques was a private establishment dedicated to children and teens with paralysis and spinal injuries, a place between hospital and home. Anny volunteered there every Tuesday and Thursday afternoon. She had done it since she'd come to Cannes to work on her doctoral dissertation right after Christmas five months ago.

At first she'd gone simply to be useful and to do something besides write about prehistoric cave painting all day. It got her out of the flat. And it was public service—something princesses did.

She loved children, and spending a few hours with ones whose lives were often severely limited seemed like time well-spent. But what had started out as a distraction and a good deed quickly turned into the time she looked forward to most each week.

At the clinic she wasn't a princess. The children had no idea who she was. And when she came to see them it wasn't a duty. It was a joy. She was simply Anny—their friend.

She played catch with Paul and video games with Madeleine and Charles. She watched football with Philippe and Gabriel and sewed tiny dolls' clothes with Marie-Claire. She talked movies and movie stars with eager starry-eyed Elise and argued—about everything—with "cranky Franck," the resident fifteen-year-old cynic who challenged her at every turn. She looked forward to it.

"I'm always at the clinic until five at least," she'd protested to her father this morning. "Gerard can meet me there."

"Gerard will not visit hospitals."

"It's a clinic," Anny protested.

"Even so. He will not," her father said firmly, but there was a sympathetic note in his voice. "You know that. Not since Ofelia…"

He didn't finish. He didn't have to.

Ofelia was Gerard's wife.

Had been Gerard's wife, Anny had corrected herself. Until her death four years ago. Now beautiful, charming, elegant Ofelia was the woman Anny was supposed to replace.

"Of course," she'd said quietly. "I forgot."

"We must understand," her father said gently. "It is hard for him, Adriana."

"I do understand."

She understood that there was every likelihood she'd never replace Ofelia in Gerard's affections. She only knew she was supposed to try. And that was at least part of the reason she was feeling apprehensive.

"He'll meet you in the lobby at five. You will have an early dinner and discuss," her father went on. "Then he must leave for Paris. He has a flight in the morning to Montreal. Business meetings."

Gerard was a prince, yes, but he owned a multinational corporation—several of them, in fact—on the side.

"What does he want to discuss?" Anny asked.

"I'm sure he will tell you tonight," her father said. "You mustn't keep him waiting, my dear."

"No."

She hadn't kept him waiting. It was Gerard who wasn't here.

Now Anny did tap her foot. Just once. Well, maybe twice. And she shot another surreptitious glance at her watch, while in her head her father's voice murmured, "Princesses are not impatient."

Maybe not, but it was already almost quarter til six. She could have stayed at the clinic and finished her argument with Franck about the relative merits of realism in television action hero series after all.

Instead, when she'd had to leave early, he'd accused her of "running away."

"I am not 'running away'!" Anny told him. "I have to meet my fiancé this afternoon."

"Fiancé?" Franck had frowned at her from beneath his mop of untidy brown hair. "You're getting married? When?"

"In a year. Maybe two. I'm not sure." Sometime in the foreseeable future no doubt. Gerard needed an heir and he wasn't prepared to wait forever.

He had agreed to wait until she had finished her dissertation. Barring disaster, that would be sometime next year. Not long.

Not long enough.

She shoved the thought away. It wasn't as if Gerard was some horrible ogre her father was forcing her to marry. Well, yes, he'd arranged it, but there was nothing wrong with Gerard. He was kind, he was thoughtful. He was a prince—in more than one sense of the word.

It was just— Anny shook off her uneasiness and reminded herself that she was simply relieved he understood that finishing her dissertation was important to her and that he hadn't minded waiting until she had finished.

Apparently Franck did mind. He scowled, his dark eyes narrowed on her. "A year? Two? *Years*? What on earth are you waiting for?"

His question jolted her. She stared at him. "What do you mean?"

He flung out a hand, a sweeping gesture that took in the four walls, the clean but spartan clinic room, his own paralyzed legs. He stared at her, then at them, then his gaze lifted again to bore into hers.

"You never know what's going to happen, do you?" he demanded.

He had been playing soccer—going up to head a ball at the same time another boy had done the same. The next day the other boy's head was a little sore. Franck was paralyzed from the waist down. He had a bit of tingling now and then, but he hadn't walked in nearly three years.

"You shouldn't wait," he said firmly. His eyes never left hers.

It was the sort of pronouncement Franck was inclined to make, an edict handed down from on high, one designed to get her to argue with him.

That was what they did: argued. Not just about action heroes. About soccer teams. The immutable laws of science. The best desserts. In short, everything.

It was his recreation, one of the nurses had said to Anny back in January, and she'd only been marginally joking.

"So what are you saying? That you think I should run off and elope?" Anny had challenged him with a smile.

But Franck's eyes didn't light with the challenge of battle the way they usually did. They glittered, but it was a fierce glitter as he shook his head. "I just don't see why you're waiting."

"A year's not long," Anny protested. "Even two. I have to finish my doctorate. And when we do set a date there will be lots to do. Preparations." Protocol. Tradition. She didn't explain about royal weddings. Ordinary everyday weddings were demanding enough.

"Stuff you'd rather do?" Franck asked.

"That's not the point."

"Of course it is. 'Cause if it isn't, you shouldn't waste time. You should do what you want to do!"

"People can't always do what they want to do, Franck," she said gently.

He snorted. "Tell me about it!" he said bitterly. "I wouldn't be locked up in here if I didn't have to be!"

Anny felt instantly guilty for her prim preachiness. "I know that."

Franck's jaw tightened, and his fingers plucked at the bed-clothes. He pressed his lips together and turned his head away to stare out the window. He didn't say anything, and Anny didn't know what to say. She shifted from one foot to the other.

Finally he shrugged his shoulders and shifted his gaze back to look at her. "You only get one life," he said.

His voice had lost its fierceness. It was flat, toneless. His eyes had lost their glitter. His expression was bleak. And seeing it made Anny feel wretched. She wanted desperately to provoke him, to argue with him, to say it wasn't so.

But it was.

He wasn't ever going to be running down the street to meet

Gerard—or anyone else—again. And how could she argue with that?

So she did the only thing she could do. She'd reached out and gave his hand a quick hard squeeze. She had wished she could bring Gerard back with her. Meeting a prince might take his mind off his misery at least for a while. But her father was right, Gerard wouldn't come.

"I have to go," she said. "I'm sorry."

Franck's mouth had twisted. "Go, then." It was a curt dismissal. He looked away quickly, his jaw hard, his expression stony. Only the rapid blink of his lashes gave him away.

"I'll be back," Anny had promised.

She should have stayed.

Another look at her watch told her that it was ten to six now and there was still no sign of Gerard.

But the moment she glanced down at her watch, a sudden silence fell over the whole room, as if everyone in the entire lobby had stopped to draw in a single collective breath.

Startled, Anny looked up. Had they noticed her prince after all?

Certainly everyone in the room seemed to be staring at something. Anny followed their gaze.

At the sight of the man now standing at the far end of the room, her heart kicked over in her chest. All she could do was stare, too.

It wasn't Gerard.

Not even close. Gerard was smooth, refined and cosmopolitan, the personfication of continental charm, a blend of 21st century sophistication and nearly as many centuries of royal breeding.

This man was anything but. He was hard-edged, shaggy-haired, and unshaven, wearing a pair of faded jeans and a nondescript open-necked shirt. He might have been nobody. A beach bum, a carpenter, a sailor in from the sea. He seemed to be cultivating the look.

But he was Somebody—with a capital S.

His name was Demetrios Savas. Anny knew it. So did everyone else in the room.

For ten years he'd been *the* golden boy of Hollywood. A man descended from Greek immigrants to America, Demetrios had started his brilliant career as nothing more than a handsome face. And stunning body.

In his early twenties, he'd modeled underwear, for goodness' sake!

But from those inauspicious beginnings, he'd worked hard to parlay not only his looks, but also his talent into a notable acting career, a successful television series, half a dozen feature films, and a fledgling but well-respected directing career. Not to mention his brief tragic fairy-tale marriage to the beautiful talented actress Lissa Conroy.

Demetrios and Lissa had been Hollywood's—and the world's—sweethearts. One of the film industry's golden couples—extraordinarily beautiful, talented people who lived charmed lives.

Charmed at least until two years ago when Lissa had contracted some sort of infection while filming overseas and had died scant days thereafter. Demetrios, working on the other side of the globe, had barely reached her side before she was gone.

Anny remembered the news photos that had chronicled his lonely journey home with her body and the shots of the treeless windswept North Dakota cemetery where he'd taken her to be buried. She still recalled how the starkness of it shocked her.

And yet it had made sense when she'd heard his explanation. "This is where she came from. It's what she'd want. I'm just bringing her home."

In her mind's eye she could still see the pain that had etched the features of his beautiful face that day.

She hadn't seen that face since. In the two years since Lissa Conroy's death and burial, Demetrios Savas had not made a public appearance.

He'd gone to ground—somewhere. And while the tabloids had reprinted pictures of a hollow-faced grieving Demetrios at first, when he didn't return to the limelight, when there were no more sightings and no more news, eventually they'd looked elsewhere for stories.

They'd been caught off guard, then, to learn last summer that he had written a screenplay, had found backing to shoot it, had cast it and, taking cast and crew to Brazil, had directed a small independent film—a film that was getting considerable interest and possible Oscar buzz, a film he was bringing to Cannes.

And now here he was.

Anny had never seen him before in person though she had certainly seen plenty of photos—had even, heaven help her, had a very memorable poster of him on the wall of her dorm room at university.

It didn't hold a candle to the man in the flesh. The stark pain from those post-funeral photos was gone from his face now. He wasn't smiling. He didn't have to. He exuded a charisma that simply captured everyone's gaze.

He had a strength and power she recognized immediately. It wasn't the smooth, controlled power like Gerard's and her father's. It was raw and elemental. She could sense it like a force field surrounding him as he moved.

And he was moving again now, though he'd stopped for just a moment to glance back over his shoulder before he continued into the room. He had an easy commanding stride, and though princesses didn't stare, according to her father, Anny couldn't look away.

A few people had picked up their conversations again. But most were still watching him. Talking about him, too, no doubt. Some nodded to him, spoke to him, and he spared them a faint smile, a quick nod. But he didn't stop, and as he moved he scanned the room as if he were looking for someone.

And then his gaze lit on her.

Their eyes locked, and Anny was trapped in the green magic of his eyes.

It seemed to take a lifetime before she could muster her good sense and years of regal breeding and drag her gaze away. Deliberately she consulted her watch, made a point of studying it intently, allowed her impatience full rein. It was better than looking at him—staring like a besotted teenager at his craggy hard compelling face.

Where in heaven's name *was* Gerard, anyway?

She looked up desperately—and found herself staring straight into Demetrios Savas's face.

He was close enough to touch. Close enough that she could see tiny gold flecks in those impossibly green eyes, and pick out a few individual grey whiskers in rough dark stubble on his cheeks and jaw.

She opened her mouth. No sound came out.

"Sorry," he said to her, a rueful smile touching his lips. "Didn't mean to keep you waiting."

Me? she wanted to say, swallowing her serene princess smile. Surely not.

But before she could say a thing, he wrapped an arm around her and drew her into his, then pressed hard warm lips to hers.

Anny's ears buzzed. Her knees wobbled. Her lips parted. For an instant she thought his tongue touched hers!

Her eyes snapped open to stare, astonished, into his.

"Thanks for waiting." His voice was the warm rough baritone she'd heard in movies and on television. As she stared in silent amazement, he kept an arm around her waist, tucked her firmly against him and walked her briskly with him toward the shops at the far end of the lobby. "Let's get out of here."

Demetrios didn't know who she was.

He didn't care. She was obviously waiting for someone—he'd seen her scanning the room almost the moment he'd walked in— and she looked like the sort of woman who wouldn't make a fuss.

Not fussing was at the top of his list of desirable female attributes at the moment. And amid all the preening peacocks she stood out like a beacon.

Her understated appearance and neat dark upswept hair would have screamed practical, sensible, unflappable, and calm if they had been capable of screaming anything.

As it was, they spoke calmly of a woman of quiet composed sanity. One of the hotel concierge staff, probably. Or a tour guide waiting for her group. Or, hell, for all he knew, a Cub Scout den mother. In other words, she was all the things that people in the movie industry generally were not.

And she was, whether she knew it or not, going to be his salvation. She was going to get him out of the Ritz before he lost his temper or his sanity or did something he would no doubt seriously regret. In her proper dark blue skirt and casual but tailored cream-colored jacket, she looked like exactly the sort of steady unflappable professional woman he needed to pull this off.

He had his arm around her as he walked her straight down the center of the room. It was as if they were parting the seas as they went. Eyes widened. Murmurs began. He ignored them.

In her ear he said, "Do you know how to get out of here?" Even as he spoke, he realized she might not even speak English. This was France, after all.

But she didn't disappoint him. She didn't stumble as he steered her along, but kept pace with him easily, turning her head toward him just enough so that he could see a smile on her face. She had just the barest hint of an accent when she said, "Of course."

He smiled, then, too. It was probably the first real smile he'd managed all day.

"Lead the way," he murmured and, while to casual observers it would appear that he was directing their movements, he was in fact following her. The murmurs in the room seemed to grow in volume and intensity as they passed.

"Ignore them," he said.

She did, still smiling as they walked. His savior seemed to know exactly where she was going. Either that or she was used to being picked up by strange men in hotel lobbies and had a designated spot for doing away with them. She led him through a set of doors and down another long corridor. Then they passed some offices, went through a storeroom and a delivery reception area and at last, when she pushed open one more door, came to stand on the pavement outside the back of the hotel.

Demetrios took a deep breath—and heard the door lock with a decisive click behind them.

He grimaced. "And now you can't get back in. Sorry. Really. But thank you. You saved my life."

"I doubt that." But she was smiling as she said it.

"My professional life," he qualified, giving her a weary smile in return. He raked fingers through his hair. "It's been a hellish day. And it was just about to get a whole lot worse."

She gave him a speculatively raised brow, but made no comment other than to say, "Well, then I'm glad to have been of service."

"Are you?" That surprised him because she actually sounded glad and not annoyed, which she had every right to be. "You were waiting for someone."

"That's why you picked me." She said it matter-of-factly and that surprised him, too.

But he grinned at her astute evaluation of the situation. "It's called improvisation. I'm Demetrios, by the way."

"I know."

Yes, he supposed she did.

If there was one thing he'd figured out in the past forty-eight hours it was that he might have fallen off the face of the earth for the past two years, but no one seemed to have forgotten who he was.

In the industry, that was good. Distributors he wanted to talk to didn't close their doors to him. But the paparazzi's long memory he could have done without. They'd swarmed over him the moment they'd seen his face. The groupies had, too.

"What'd you expect?" his brother Theo had said sardonically. He'd dropped by Demetrios's hotel room unannounced this morning en route sailing from Spain to Santorini. He'd grinned unsympathetically. "They all want to be the one to assuage your sorrow."

Demetrios had known that coming to Cannes would be a madhouse, but he'd told himself he could manage. And he would be able to if all the women he met were like this one.

"Demetrios Savas in person," she mused now, a smile touching her lips as she studied him with deep blue eyes. She looked friendly and mildly curious, but nothing more, thank God.

"At least you're not giddy with excitement about it," he said drily with a self-deprecating grin.

"I might be." A dimple appeared in her left cheek when her smile widened. "Maybe I'm just hiding it well."

"Keep right on hiding it. Please."

She laughed at that, and he liked her laugh, too. It was warm and friendly and somehow it made her seem even prettier. She was a pretty girl. A wholesome sort of girl. Nothing theatrical or glitzy about her. Fresh and friendly with the sort of flawless complexion that cosmetic companies would kill for.

"Are you a model?" he asked, suddenly realizing she could be. And why not? She could have been waiting for an agent. A rep. It made sense. And some of them could contrive to look fresh and wholesome.

God knew Lissa had.

But this woman actually looked surprised at his question. "A model? No. Not at all. Do I look like one?" She laughed then, as if it were the least likely thing she could think of.

"You could be," he told her.

"Really?" She looked sceptical, then shrugged "Well, thank you. I think." She dimpled again as she smiled at him.

"I just meant you're beautiful. It was a compliment. Do you work for the hotel then?"

"Beautiful?" That seemed to surprise her, too. But she didn't dwell on it. "No, I don't work there. Do I look like I could do that, too?" The smile that played at the corners of her mouth made him grin.

"You look…hospitable. Casually professional." His gaze slid over her more slowly this time, taking in the neat upswept dark brown hair and the creamy complexion with its less-is-more makeup before moving on to the curves beneath the tastefully tailored jacket and skirt, the smooth, slender tanned legs, the toes peeking out from her sandals. "Attractive," he said. "Approachable."

"Approachable?"

"I approached," he pointed out.

"You make me sound like a streetwalker." But she didn't sound offended, just amused.

But Demetrios shook his head. "Never. You're not wearing enough makeup. And the clothes are all wrong."

"Well, that's a relief."

They smiled at each other again, and quite suddenly Demetrios felt as if he were waking up from a bad dream.

He'd been in it so long—dragged down and fighting his way back—that it seemed as if it would be all he'd ever know for the rest of his life.

But right now, just this instant, he felt alive. And he realized that he had smiled more—really honestly smiled—in the past five minutes than he had in the past three years.

"What's your name?" he asked.

"Anny."

Anny. A plain name. A first name. No last name. Usually women were falling all over themselves to give him their full names, the story of their lives, and, most importantly, their phone numbers.

"Just Anny?" he queried lightly.

"Chamion." She seemed almost reluctant to tell him. That was refreshing.

"Anny Chamion." He liked the sound of it. Simple. But a little exotic. "You're French?"

"My mother was French."

"And you speak English perfectly."

"I went to university in the States. Well, I went to Oxford first. But I went to graduate school in California. At Berkeley. I still am, really. I'm working on my dissertation."

"So, you're a...scholar?"

She didn't look like any scholar he'd ever met. No pencils in her hair. There was nothing distracted or ivory towerish about her. He knew all about scholarly single-mindedness. His brother George was a scholar—a physicist.

"You're not a physicist?" he said accusingly.

She laughed. "Afraid not. I'm an archaeologist."

He grinned. "*Raiders of the Lost Ark*? My brothers and I used to watch that over and over."

Anny nodded, her eyes were smiling. Then she shrugged wryly. "The 'real' thing isn't quite so exciting."

"No Nazis and gun battles?"

"Not many snakes, either. And not a single dashing young Harrison Ford. I'm working on my dissertation right now—on cave paintings. No excitement there, either. But I like it. I've done the research. It's just a matter of getting it all organized and down on paper."

"Getting stuff down on paper isn't always easy." It had been perhaps the hardest part of the past couple of years, mostly because it required that he be alone with his thoughts.

"You're writing a dissertation?"

"A screenplay," he said. "I wrote one. Now I'm starting another. It's hard work."

"All that creativity would be exhausting. I couldn't do it," she said with admiration.

"I couldn't write a dissertation." He should just thank her and say goodbye. But he liked her. She was sane, normal, sensible, smart. Not a starlet. Not even remotely. It was nice to be with someone unrelated to the movie business. Unrelated to the hoopla and glitz. Down-to-earth. He was oddly reluctant to simply walk away.

"Have dinner with me," he said abruptly.

Her eyes widened. Her mouth opened. Then it closed.

Practically every other woman in Cannes, Demetrios thought grimly, would have said yes ten times over by now.

Not Anny Chamion. She looked rueful, then gave him a polite shake of the head. "I would love to, but I'm afraid I really was waiting for someone in the hotel."

Of course she had been.

"And I just shanghaied you without giving a damn." He grimaced. "Sorry. I just thought it would be nice to find a little hole-in-the-wall place, hide out for a while. Have a nice meal. Some conversation. I forgot I'd kidnapped you under false pretenses."

She laughed. "It's all right. He was late."

He. Of course she was waiting for a man. And what difference did it make?

"Right," he said briskly. "Thanks for the rescue, Anny Chamion. I didn't offend Mona Tremayne because of you."

"The actress?" She looked startled. "You were escaping from her?"

"Not her. Her daughter. Rhiannon. She's a little…persistent." She'd been following him around since yesterday morning, telling him she'd make him forget.

Anny raised her brows. "I see."

"She's a nice girl. A bit intense. Immature." And way too determined. "I don't want to tell her to get lost. I'd like to work with her mother again…."

"It was truly a diplomatic maneuver."

He nodded. "But I'm sorry if I messed something up for you."

"Don't worry about it." She held out a hand in farewell, and he took it, held it. Her fingers were soft and smooth and warm. He ran his thumb over them.

"I kissed you before," he reminded her.

"Ah, but you didn't know me then."

"Still—" It surprised him how much he wanted to do it again.

But before he could make his move, she jerked, surprised, and stuck her hand into the pocket of her jacket.

"My phone," she said apologetically, taking it out and glancing at the ID. "I wouldn't answer it. It's rude. I'm so sorry. It's—" She waved a hand toward the hotel from which they'd come. "I need to get this."

Because it was obviously from the man she'd been waiting for. His mouth twisted, but he shrugged equably. "Of course. No problem. It's been—"

He stopped because he couldn't find the right word. What had it been? A pleasure? Yes, it had been. And real. It had been "real." For the first time in three years he'd felt, for a few brief moments, as if he had solid ground under his feet. He squeezed her hand, then leaned in and kissed her firmly on the mouth. "Thank you, Anny Chamion."

Her eyes widened in shock.

He smiled. Then for good measure, he kissed her again, and enjoyed every moment of it, pleased, he supposed, that he hadn't entirely lost his touch.

The phone vibrated in her hand long and hard before she had the presence of mind to answer it in rapid French.

Demetrios didn't wait. He gave her a quick salute, pulled dark glasses out of his pocket, stuck them on his face, then turned and headed down the street. He had gone less than a block when he heard the sound of quick footsteps running after him.

Oh, hell. Was there no getting away from Rhiannon Tremayne?

He badly wanted Mona for a part in his next picture. To get her, he couldn't alienate her high-strung, high-maintenance, highly spoiled daughter. But he was tired, he was edgy and, having the sweet taste of Anny Chamion on his lips, he didn't relish being thrown to the jackals again. He spun around to tell her so—in the politest possible terms.

"I seem to have the evening free." It was Anny smiling, that dimple creasing her cheek again as she fell into step beside him. "So I wondered, is that dinner invitation still open?"

CHAPTER TWO

PRINCESSES DIDN'T INVITE themselves out to dinner!

They didn't say no one minute and run after a man to say yes the next. But she'd been given a reprieve, hadn't she? The phone call had been from Gerard, who was going straight to Paris to get a good night's sleep before his flight to Montreal.

"I'll see you on my way back," he'd said. "Next week. We need to talk."

Anny had never understood what people thought they were doing on the phone if not talking, but she said politely, "Of course. I'll look forward to seeing you then."

She hung up almost before Gerard could say goodbye, because if she didn't start running now, she might lose sight of Demetrios when he reached the corner. She'd never run after a man in her life. And she knew perfectly well she shouldn't be chasing one now.

But how often did Demetrios Savas invite her out to dinner— at the very moment her prince decided not to show up?

If that didn't confirm the universe's benevolence, what did?

Besides, it was only dinner, after all. A meal. An hour or two.

But with Demetrios Savas. The fulfillment of a youthful dream. How many women got invited to dinner by the man whose poster they'd had on the wall at age eighteen?

As a tribute to that idealistic dreamy girl, Anny couldn't *not* do it.

He spun around as she reached him, his jaw tight, his eyes hard. It was that same fierce look that had made his name a household word when he'd played rough-edged bad-ass spy Luke St. Angier on American television seven or eight years ago.

Anny stopped dead.

Then at the sight of her, the muscles in his jaw eased. And she was, quite suddenly, rewarded by the very grin that had had thousands—no, *millions*—of girls and women and little old ladies falling at his feet.

"Anny." Her name on his lips sent her heart to hammering. "Change your mind?" he asked with just the right hopeful note.

"If you don't mind." She wasn't sure if her breathlessness was due to the man in front of her who was, admittedly, pretty breathtaking, or to her own sudden out-of-character seizing of the moment.

"Mind?" Demetrios's memorable grin broadened. "As if. So?" He cocked his head. "Yes?"

"I don't want to presume," she said as demurely as possible.

"Go ahead and presume." He grinned as he glanced around the busy street scene. Then his grin faded as he realized how many people were beginning to notice him. One of a gaggle of teenage girls pointed in their direction. Another gave a tiny high-pitched scream, and instantly they cut across the street to head his way.

For an instant he looked like a fox with the hounds baying as they closed in. But only for a moment.

Then he said, "Hang on, will you? I'm sorry but—"

"I understand," Anny replied quickly. No one understood better the demands of the public than someone raised to be a princess. Duty to her public had been instilled in her from the time she was born.

That hadn't been the case for Demetrios, of course. He'd become famous in his early twenties, and as far as she knew he'd had no preparation at all for how to deal with it. Still, he'd always handled fame well. Even in the tragic circumstances of his wife's death, he'd been composed and polite. And while he might have gone to ground afterward, as far as Anny was concerned, he'd had every right.

He'd come back when he was ready, obviously. And while he clearly hadn't sought this swarm of fans, he welcomed them easily, smiling at them as they surged across the street toward him

Confident of their welcome, they chattered and giggled as they crowded around. And Demetrios let them envelop him, jostle him as he laughed and talked with them in Italian, for that was what they spoke.

It wasn't good Italian. Anny knew that because she spoke it perfectly. But he made the effort, stumbled over his words and kept on trying. If the girls hadn't already been enchanted, they would be now.

And watching him, listening to him, Anny was more than a bit enchanted herself.

Of course he'd been gorgeous as a young man. But she found him even more appealing now. His youthful handsome face had matured. His cheekbones were sharper, his jaw harder and stronger. The rough stubble gave him a more mature version of the roguish look he'd only begun to develop in the years he'd played action hero Luke St. Angier. Hard at work on her university courses, Anny had rarely taken the time to watch anything on television. But she had always watched him.

Demetrios Savas had been her indulgence.

Looking at him now, admiring his good looks, mesmerizing eyes, and easy grin, as well as that enticing groove in his cheek that appeared whenever the grin did, it wasn't hard to remember why.

But it wasn't only his stunning good looks that appealed. It was the way he interacted with his ever-so-eager fans.

He might have run from the sharklike pursuit of some intense desperate starlet, but he was kind to these girls who wanted nothing more than a smile and a few moments of conversation with their Hollywood hero.

Actually "kind" didn't begin to cover it. He actually seemed "interested," and he focused on each one—not just the cute, flirty ones. He talked to them all, listened to them all. Laughed with them. Made them feel special.

That impressed her. She wondered where he'd learned it or if it came naturally. Whichever, it didn't seem to bother him. Somehow he'd learned the very useful skill of turning the tables and making the meeting all about them, not him. For once she got to simply lean against the outside wall of one of the shops and enjoy the moment.

It was odd, really. She'd barely thought of him in years. Responsibilities had weighed, duties had demanded. She'd fulfilled them all. And she'd let her girlish fantasies fall by the wayside.

Now she thought, *I'm having dinner with Demetrios Savas*, and almost laughed at the giddy feeling of pleasure at the prospect. It was as heady as it was unlikely.

She wondered what Gerard would say if she told him.

Actually she suspected she knew. He would blink and then he would look down his regal nose and ask politely, "Who?"

Or maybe she was selling him short. Maybe he did know who Demetrios was. But he certainly wouldn't expect his future wife to be having dinner with him. Not that he would care. Or feel threatened.

Of course he had no reason to feel threatened. It wasn't as if Demetrios was going to sweep her off her feet and carry her away with him.

All the while she was musing, though, the crowd around him, rather than dissipating, was getting bigger. Demetrios was still talking, answering questions, charming them all, but his gaze flicked around now and lit on her. He raised his brows as if to say, *What can I do?*

Anny shrugged and smiled. Another half a dozen questions and the crowd seemed to double again. His gaze found her again and this time he mouthed a single word in her direction. "Taxi?"

She nodded and began scanning the street. When she had nearly decided that the only way to get one was to go back to the Ritz-Carlton, an empty one appeared at the corner. She sprinted toward it.

"Demetrios!"

He glanced up, saw the cab, offered smiles and a thousand apologies to his gathered fans, then managed to slip after her into the cab.

"Sorry," he said. "Sometimes it's a little insane."

"I can see that," she said.

"It goes with the territory," he said. "And usually they mean well. They're interested. They care. I appreciate that." He shrugged. "And in effect they pay my salary. I owe them." He flexed his shoulders against the seat back tiredly. "And when it's about my work, it's fine. Sometimes it's not." His gaze seemed to close up for a moment, but then he was back, rubbing a hand through his hair. "Sometimes it's a little overwhelming."

"Especially when you've been away from it for a while."

He gave her a sharp speculative look, and she wondered if she'd overstepped her bounds. But then he shrugged. "Especially when I've been away from it for a while," he acknowledged.

The driver, who had been waiting patiently, caught her gaze in the rearview mirror and asked where they wanted to go.

Demetrios obviously knew enough French to get by, too, because he understood and asked her, "Where do we want to go? Some place that's not a madhouse, preferably."

"Are you hungry now?" Anny asked.

"Not really. Just in no mood to deal with paparazzi. Know any place quiet?"

She nodded. "For dinner, yes. A little place in Le Soquet, the old quarter, that is basically off the tourist track." She looked at him speculatively, an idea forming. "You don't want to talk to anyone?"

A brow lifted. "I want to talk to you."

Enchanted, Anny smiled. "Flatterer." He was amazingly charming. "I was thinking, if you're really not hungry yet, but you wouldn't mind talking to a few more kids—not paparazzi, not journalists—just kids who would love to meet you—"

"You have kids?" he said, startled.

Quickly Anny shook her head. "No. I volunteer at a clinic for children and teenagers with spinal injuries and paralysis. I was there this afternoon. And I was having a sort of discussion—well, argument, really, with one of the boys…he's a teenager—about action heroes."

Demetrios's mouth quirked. "You argue about action heroes?"

"Franck will pretty much argue about anything. He likes to argue. And he has opinions."

"And you do, too?" There was a teasing light in his eye now.

Anny smiled. "I suppose I do," she admitted. "But I try not to batter people with them. Except for Franck," she added. "Because it's all the recreation he gets these days. Anything I say, he takes the opposite view."

"He must have brothers," Demetrios said wryly.

But Anny shook her head. "He's an only child."

"Even worse."

"Yes." Anny thought so, too. She had been an only child herself for twenty years. Her mother had not been able to have more children after Anny, and she'd died when Anny was twelve. Only when her father married Charlise seven years ago had Anny dared to hope for a sibling.

Now she had three little half brothers, Alexandre, Raoul, and David. And even though she was much older—actually old enough to be their mother—she still relished the joy of having brothers.

"Franck makes up for it by arguing with me," she said. "And I was just thinking, what a coup it would be if I brought you back to the clinic. You obviously know more about action heroes than I do so you could argue with him. Then after, we could have dinner?"

It was presumptuous. He might turn her down cold.

But somehow she wasn't surprised when he actually sat up straighter and said, "Sounds like a deal. Let's go."

The look on Franck's face when they walked into his room was priceless. His jaw went slack. No sound came out of his mouth at all.

Anny tried not to smile as she turned back toward Demetrios. "I want you to meet a friend of mine," she said to him. "This is Franck Villiers. Franck, this is—"

"I know who he is." But Franck still stared in disbelief.

Demetrios stuck out his hand. "Pleased to meet you," he said in French.

For a moment, Franck didn't take it. Then, when he did, he stared at the hand he was shaking as if the sight could convince him that the man with Anny was real.

Slowly he turned an accusing gaze on Anny "You're going to marry *him*?"

She jerked. "No!" She felt her cheeks flame.

"You said you had to leave early because you were going to meet your fiancé."

Oh God, she'd forgotten that.

"He got delayed," Anny said quickly. "He couldn't come." She shot a look at Demetrios.

He raised his brows in silent question, but he simply said to Franck, "So I invited her to dinner instead."

Franck shoved himself up farther against the pillows and looked at her. "You never said you knew Luke St. Angier. I mean—*him*," he corrected himself, cheeks reddening as if he'd embarrassed himself by confusing the man and the role he'd played.

Demetrios didn't seem to care. "We just met," he said. "Anny mentioned your discussion. I can't believe you think MacGyver is smarter than Luke St. Angier."

Anny almost laughed as Franck's gaze snapped from Demetrios to her and back again. Then his spine stiffened. "Could Luke St. Angier make a bomb out of a toaster, half a dozen toothpicks and a cigarette lighter?"

"Damn right he could," Demetrios shot back. "Obviously we need to talk."

Maybe it was because he, like Anny, treated Franck no differently than he would treat anybody else, maybe it was because he was Luke St. Angier, whatever it was, the next thing Anny knew Demetrios was sitting on the end of Franck's bed and the two of them were going at it.

They did argue. First about bomb-making, then about scripts and character arcs and story lines. Demetrios was as intent and focused with Franck as he had been with the girls.

Anny had thought they might spend a half an hour there—at

most. Franck usually became disgruntled after that long. But not with Demetrios. They were still talking and arguing an hour later. They might have gone on all night if Anny hadn't finally said, "I hate to break this up, but we have a few more people to see here before we leave."

Franck scowled.

Demetrios stood up and said, "Okay. We can continue this tomorrow."

Franck stared. "Tomorrow? You mean it?"

"Of course I mean it," Demetrios assured him. "No one else has cared about Luke that much in years."

Franck's eyes shone. He looked over at Anny as they were going out the door and he said something she thought she would never hear him say. "Thanks."

She thanked Demetrios, too, when they were out in the hall again. "You made his day. You don't have to come back. I can explain if you don't."

He shook his head. "I'm coming back. Now let's meet the rest of the gang."

Naturally he charmed them, one and all. And even though many of them didn't know the famous man who was with Anny, they loved the attention. Just as he had with Franck and with the Italian girls, Demetrios focused on what they were telling him. He talked about toy cars with eight-year-old François. He listened to tales about Olivia's kitten. He did his "one and only card trick" for several of the older girls. And if they weren't madly in love with Demetrios Savas when he came into their rooms, they were well on the way by the time he left.

Anny, for all her youthful fantasies about Demetrios Savas, had never really imagined him with children. Now she thought it was a shame he didn't have his own.

It was past nine-thirty when they finally stepped back out onto the narrow cobbled street in Le Soquet and Anny said guiltily, "I didn't mean to tie up your whole evening."

"If I hadn't wanted to be there," he said firmly, "I could have figured out how to leave." He took hold of her hand, turning her so that she looked into those mesmerizing eyes. She couldn't see the color now as the sun had gone down. But the intensity was there in them and in his voice when he said, "Believe me, Anny."

How could she not?

She wetted her lips. "Yes, well, thank you. It hardly seems adequate, but—"

"It's perfectly adequate. You're welcome. More than. Now, how about dinner?"

"Are you sure? It's getting late."

"Not midnight yet. In case you turn into a pumpkin," he added, his grin flashing.

Was she Cinderella then? Not ordinarily. But tonight she almost felt like it. Or the flipside thereof—the princess pretending to be a "real" person.

"No," she said, "I don't. At least I haven't yet," she added with a smile.

"I'm glad to hear it." Then his voice gentled. "Are you having second thoughts, Anny? Afraid the missing fiancé will find out?"

He still held her hand in his, and if she tugged it, she would be making too much of things. She swallowed. "He wouldn't care," she said offhandedly. "He's not that sort of man."

He cocked his head. "Is that good?"

Was it good? Anny knew she didn't want a jealous husband. But she did want a husband to whom she mattered, who loved her, who cared. On one level, of course, Gerard did.

"He's a fine man," she said at last.

"I'm sure he is," Demetrios said gravely. "So if I promise to behave in exemplary fashion with his fiancée, will you have dinner with me?"

He held her hand—and her gaze—effortlessly as he hung the invitation, the temptation, dangling there between them. He'd already asked before. She'd said no, then yes. And now?

"Yes," she said firmly. "I would like that."

She wasn't sure that she should have liked the frisson of awareness she felt when he gave her fingers a squeeze before he released them. "So would I."

* * *

He wanted to keep holding her hand.

How stupid was that?

He wasn't a besotted teenager. He was an adult. Sane, sensible. And decidedly gun-shy. Or woman-shy.

Which wasn't a problem here, Demetrios reminded himself sharply, determinedly tucking his hands in his pockets as he walked with Anny Chamion through the narrow steep streets of the Old Quarter. She was engaged and thus, clearly, no more interested in anything beyond dinner than he was.

Still, the desire unnerved him. He'd had no wish to hold any woman's hand—or even touch one—in over two years.

But ever since he'd kissed Anny Chamion that afternoon, something had awakened in him that he'd thought stone-cold dead.

Discovering it wasn't jolted him.

For as long as he could remember, Demetrios had been aware of, attracted to, charmed by women. He'd always been able to charm them as well.

"They're like bowling pins," his brother George had grumbled when they were teenagers. "He smiles at them and they topple over at his feet."

"Eat your heart out," Demetrios had laughed, always enjoying the girls, the giggles, the adulation.

It had only grown when, after college where he'd studied film, he'd taken an offer of a modeling job as a way to bring in some money while he tried to land acting roles. The modeling helped. His face became familiar and, as one director said, "They don't care what you're selling. They're buying you."

The directors had bought him. So had the public. They had found him even more engaging in action than in stills.

"The charisma really comes through there," all the casting directors were eager to point out. And it wasn't long before he was not just doing commercials and small supporting parts, he was the star of his own television series.

Three years of being Luke St. Angier got him fame, fortune, opportunities and adulation, movie scripts landing on his doorstep, plus all the women he would ever want, including the one he did—the gorgeous and talented actress, Lissa Conroy.

The last woman he had felt a stab of desire for. The last one he'd cared for. The last one he would ever let himself care for.

But this had nothing to do with caring. This was pure masculine desire confronted with a beautiful woman. He couldn't expect his hormones to stay dormant forever, he supposed, though it had been easier when they had.

He glanced up to see that the distraction herself had stepped over to talk to the waiter in a small restaurant where they'd stopped. The place was, as she'd promised, no more than a hole in the wall. It had a few tables inside and four more, filled with diners, on the pavement in front.

She finished talking to the waiter and came back to him. "They know me here. The food is good. The moussaka is fantastic. And it's not exactly on the tourist path. They have a table near the kitchen. Not exactly the best seat in the house. So if you would prefer somewhere else…"

Demetrios shook his head. "It's fine."

And if not perfect because the table really was right outside the kitchen door, no one paid any attention to them there. No one expected a film star to sit at the least appealing table in the place, so no one glanced at him. The cook and waiter were far too busy to care who they fed, but even though they seemed run off their feet, they doted on Anny. Menus appeared instantly. A wine list quickly followed.

"You come here often?"

"When I don't cook for myself, I come here. They have great food." And she ordered the bouillabaisse without even looking at anything else. "It's always wonderful."

He was tempted. But he was more tempted by the moussaka she had mentioned earlier. No one made it like his mother. But he hadn't been home in almost three years. Had barely talked to his parents since he'd seen them after Lissa's funeral. Had kept them at a distance the entire year before.

He knew they didn't understand. And he couldn't explain.

Couldn't make them understand about Lissa when he didn't even understand himself. And after—after he couldn't face them. Not yet.

So it was easier to stay away.

At least until he'd come to terms on his own.

So he had. He was back, wasn't he? He had a new screenplay with his name on it. He had a new film. He'd brought it to Cannes, the most public and prestigious of film festivals. He was out in public, doing interviews, charming fans, smiling for all he was worth.

And tonight moussaka sounded good. Smelled good, too, he thought as he detected the scent mingling with other aromas in the kitchen. It reminded him of his youth, of happier times. The good old days.

Maybe after he was finished at Cannes, he'd go see Theo and Martha and their kids in Santorini, then fly back to the States and visit his folks.

He ordered the moussaka, then looked up to see Anny smiling at him.

"What?" he said.

She shook her head. "Just bemused," she told him. "Surprised that I'm here. With you."

"Fate," he said, tasting the wine the waiter brought, then nodding his approval.

"Do you believe that?"

"No. But I'm a screenwriter, too. I like turning points." It was glib and probably not even true. God knew some of the turning points in his life had been disasters even if on the screen they were useful. But Anny seemed struck by the notion.

The waiter poured her wine. She looked up and thanked him, earning her a bright smile in return. Then she picked it up and sipped it contemplatively, her expression serious.

He wanted to see her smile again. "So, you're writing a dissertation. You volunteer at a clinic. You have a fiancé. You went to Oxford. And Berkeley. Tell me more. What else should I know about Anny Chamion?"

She hesitated, as if she weren't all that comfortable talking about herself, which was in itself refreshing.

Lissa had commanded the center of attention wherever they'd been. But Anny spread her palms and shrugged disingenuously, then shocked him by saying, "I had a poster of you on my wall when I was eighteen."

Demetrios groaned and put his hand over his eyes. He knew the poster. It was an artistic, tasteful, nonrevealing nude, which he'd done at the request of a young photographer friend trying to make a name for herself.

She had.

So had he. His brothers and every male friend he'd ever had, seeing that poster, had taunted him about it for years. Still did. His parents, fortunately, had had a sense of humor and had merely rolled their eyes. Girls seemed to like it, though.

"I was young and dumb," he admitted now, ruefully shaking his head.

"But gorgeous," Anny replied with such disarming frankness that he blinked.

"Thanks," he said a little wryly. But he found her admiration oddly pleasing. It wasn't as if he hadn't heard the sentiment before, but knowing a cool, self-possessed woman like Anny had been attracted kicked the activity level of his formerly dormant hormones up another notch.

He shifted in his chair. "Tell me about something besides the poster. Tell me how you met your fiancé?" He didn't really want to know that, but it seemed like a good idea to ask, remind his hormones of the reality of the situation.

The waiter set salads in front of them. Demetrios picked up his fork.

"I've known him all my life," Anny said.

"The boy next door?"

"Not quite. But, well, sort of."

"Helps if you know someone well." God knew it would have helped if he'd known more about what made Lissa tick. It would have sent him running in the other direction. But how could he have when she was so good at playing a role? "You know him, at least."

"Yes." This time her smile didn't seem to reach her eyes. She focused on her salad, not offering any more so Demetrios changed the subject.

"Tell me about these cave paintings. How much more work do you have to do on your dissertation?"

She was more forthcoming about that. She talked at length about her work and her eyes lit up then. Ditto when he got her talking about the clinic and the children.

He found her enthusiasm contagious, and when she asked him about the film he'd brought to Cannes, he shared some of his own enthusiasm.

She was a good listener. She asked good questions. Even better, she knew what not to ask. She said nothing at all about the two plus years he'd stayed out of the public eye. Nothing about his marriage. Nothing about Lissa's death.

Only when he brought up not having come to Cannes for a couple of years did she say simply, "I was sorry to hear about your wife."

"Thank you."

They got through the salad, their entrées—the moussaka was remarkably good and reminiscent of his mother's—and then, because Anny looked a second or so too long at the apple tart, and because he really didn't want the evening to end yet, he suggested they share a piece with their coffee.

"Just a bite for me," she agreed. "I eat far too much of it whenever I come here."

Demetrios liked that she had enjoyed her meal. He liked that she wasn't rail-thin and boney the way Lissa had been, the way so many actresses felt they needed to be. She hadn't picked at her food the way they did. She looked healthy and appealing— just right, in his estimation—with definite hints of curves beneath her tailored jacket, scoop-necked top and linen skirt.

The hormones were definitely awake.

The waiter brought the apple tart and two forks. And

Demetrios was almost annoyed to discover he wasn't going to be able to feed her a bite off his. *Almost*.

Then sanity reared its head. He got a grip, pushed the plate toward her. "After you."

She cut off a small piece and carried it to her mouth, then shut her eyes and sighed. "That is simply heaven." She ran her tongue lightly over her lips, and opened her eyes again.

"Taste it," she urged him.

His hormones heard, *Taste me*. He cleared his throat and focused on the tart.

It was good. He did his best to savor it appreciatively, aware of her eyes on him, watching him as he chewed and swallowed.

"Your turn."

She shook her head. "One bite. That's it."

"It's heaven," he reminded her.

"I've had my taste for tonight." She set down her fork and put her hands in her lap. "Truly. Please, finish it."

He took his time, not just to savor the tart but the evening as well. It was the first time he'd been out on anything remotely resembling a date since Lissa. Not that this was precisely a date. He wasn't doing dates—not ones that led anywhere except bed now that his hormones were awake and kicking.

Still he was enjoying himself. This was a step back into the normal world he'd left three years before, made easier because of the woman Anny was…comfortable, poised, appealing. He liked her ease and her calmness at the same time he felt a renegade impulse to ruffle that calm.

The notion brought him up short. Where the hell had *that* come from?

He forked the last bite into his mouth and washed it down with a quick swallow of coffee.

Anny shook her head in gentle sadness. "You weren't treating it like heaven just then."

He wiped his mouth on the napkin, then dropped it on the table. "I realized I was making you wait. It's nearly midnight," he said, surprised at how the time had flown.

"Maybe I will turn into a pumpkin." She didn't smile when she said it.

He did. "Can I watch?"

"Prince Charming is always long gone when that happens, remember?"

He remembered. And he remembered, too, that however enjoyable it had been, unlike the Cinderella story, it wasn't going anywhere. He didn't want it to. She didn't want it to. That was probably what made it so damn enjoyable.

"Ready to go?"

She nodded. She looked remote now, a little pensive.

He paid the bill, told the waiter what a great meal it was, and was bemused when the waiter barely looked at him, but had a smile for Anny. "We are so happy to have you come tonight, your— You're always welcome." He even kissed her hand.

Outside she stopped and offered that same hand to him. "Thank you. For the dinner. For coming to the clinic. For everything. It was a memorable evening."

He took her hand, but he shook his head. "I'm not leaving you on a street corner."

"My flat's not far. You don't need—"

"I'm walking you home. To your door." In case she had any other ideas. "So lead on."

He could have let go of her hand then. He didn't. He kept her fingers firmly wrapped in his as he walked beside her through the narrow streets.

In the distance he could still hear traffic moving along La Croisette. There was music from bars, an occasional motorcycle. Next to him, Anny walked in silence, her fingers warm in his palm. She didn't speak at all, and that, in itself, was a lovely novelty. Every girl he'd ever been with, from Jenny Sorensen in ninth grade to Lissa, had talked his ear off all the way to the door.

Anny didn't say a thing until she stopped in front of an old stuccoed four-story apartment building with tall shuttered French doors that opened onto narrow wrought-iron railed balconies.

"Here we are." She slipped out a key, opened the big door.

He expected she would tell him he could leave then, but she must have understood he meant the door to her own flat, because she led the way through a small spare open area to a staircase that climbed steeply up the center of the building. She pressed a light switch to illuminate the stairs and, without glancing his way, started up them.

Demetrios stayed a step behind her until they arrived at the door to her flat. She unlocked hers, then turned to offer him a smile and her hand.

"My door," she said with a smile. Then, "Thank you," she added simply. "It's been lovely."

"It has." And he meant it. It was quite honestly the loveliest night he'd had in years. "I lucked out when I commandeered you at the Ritz."

"So did I." Her eyes were luminous, like deep blue pools.

They stared at each other. The moment lingered. So did they.

Demetrios knew exactly what he should do: give her hand a polite shake, then let go of it and say goodbye. Or maybe give her a kiss. After all, he'd greeted her with a kiss before he even knew who she was.

But now he did know. She was a sweet, kind, warm young woman—who was engaged to someone else. The last sort of woman he should be lusting after.

But even knowing it, he leaned in and touched his lips to hers.

Just a taste. What the hell was wrong with a taste? He wasn't going to do anything about it.

Just…taste.

And this one couldn't be like the first time he'd kissed her. That had been for show—all determination and possession and public display.

Or like the second when he'd left her on the street corner with her phone buzzing in her hand. One quick defiant kiss because he couldn't help himself.

This time he could certainly help himself. But he didn't, because he wanted it.

He wanted to taste her. Savor her. Remember her.

And so slowly and deliberately he took Anny's lips with his.

She tasted of wine and apple and a sweetness that could only be Anny herself. He savored it more than he'd savored the tart. Couldn't seem to stop himself, like a parched man after years in the desert given the clearest most refreshing water in the world.

He would have stopped if she'd resisted, if she'd put her hands against his chest and pushed him away.

But she put her hands against his chest and hung on—clutched his shirt as if she would never let go.

He didn't know which of them was more surprised. Or which of them stepped back first.

His hormones were having a field day. After so long asleep, they were definitely wide-awake and raring to go.

Demetrios tried to ignore them, but he couldn't quite ignore the hammer of his heart against the wall of his chest, or keep his voice steady as he said, "Good night, Anny Chamion."

For a moment she just looked stunned. She barely managed a smile as she swallowed and said, "Good night."

There was another silence. Then he tipped her chin up with a single finger, and leaned down to give her one last light chaste kiss on the lips—the proper farewell kiss he should have given her moments ago.

"I owe you," he said.

She blinked. "What?"

"You rescued me, remember?"

She shook her head. "You fed me dinner. You went to see Franck."

And you brought the first evening of joy into my life in the last three years. Of course he didn't say that. He only repeated, "I owe you, Anny Chamion. If there's ever anything I can do for you, just ask."

She stared at him mutely.

He reached in his pocket and pulled out a business card, then scrawled his private number on it, tucking it into her hand. "Whatever you need. Whenever. You only have to ask. Okay?"

She nodded, her eyes wide and almighty enticing. She had no idea.

"Good night," he said firmly, deliberately—as much to convince his hormones as to say farewell to her. But he waited for her to go inside and shut the door. Only when she had did he turn and walk toward the stairs.

He had just reached them when the door jerked open behind him.

"Demetrios?" she called his name softly.

He stiffened, then turned. "What?"

He waited as she came toward him until she stood bare inches away, close enough that he could again catch the scent of the apple tart, of a faint hint of citrus shampoo.

Her eyes were wide as she looked up at him. "Anything?"

"What?" He blinked, confused.

"You said you'd do anything?"

He nodded. "Yes."

She wetted her lips. "Whatever I ask?"

"Yes," he said firmly.

"Make love with me."

CHAPTER THREE

SHE COULDN'T BELIEVE she'd said the words. Not out loud.

Thought them, yes. Wished they would come true, absolutely. But ask a man—this man!—to make love with her?

No! She couldn't have.

But one look at his face told her that, in fact, she had. Oh, dear God. She desperately wanted to recall the request. Her face burned. Her brain—provided she had one, which seemed unlikely given what she'd just done—was likely going up in smoke.

What on earth had possessed her?

Some demon no doubt. Certainly it wasn't the spirit of generations of Mont Chamion royalty. They were doubtless spinning in their graves.

"I'm sorry. I didn't mean—" She had always thought people who fanned themselves were silly and pretentious. Now she understood the impulse. She started to back away.

But Demetrios caught her hand. "You didn't mean…?" Those green eyes bored into hers.

She tried to pull away. He let go, but his gaze still held her. "I…never should have said it." She wanted to say she didn't mean it, but that wasn't true, so she didn't say that.

"You're getting married," he said quietly.

She swallowed, then nodded once, a jerky nod. "Yes."

"And you'd have meaningless sex with me before you do?"

That stung, but she shook her head. "It wouldn't be meaningless. Not to me."

"Why? Because you had my poster on your wall? Because I'm some damned movie star and you think I'd be a nice notch on your bedpost?" He really was furious.

"No! It—it isn't about you," she said, trying to find the words to express the feeling that had been growing inside her all evening long. "Not really."

"No?" He looked sceptical, then challenged her. "Okay. So tell me then, what is it about?"

She took a breath. "It's what you made me remember."

His jaw set. "What's that?" He leaned back against the wall, apparently prepared to hear her out right there.

She sighed. "It's…complicated. And I—I can't stand here in the hallway and explain. My neighbors don't expect to be disturbed at this time of night."

"Then invite me in."

Which, she realized, was pretty much what she'd already done. She shrugged, then turned and led the way back down the hall and into Tante Isabelle's apartment. She nodded toward the overstuffed sofa and waved a hand toward it. "Sit down. Can I get you some coffee?"

"I don't think either of us wants coffee, Anny," he said gruffly.

"No." That was certainly true. She wanted him. Even now. Even more. Watching him prowling around Tante Isabelle's flat like some sort of panther didn't turn off her desire. In fact it only seemed to make him more appealing. She had plenty of experience dealing with heads of state, but none dealing with panthers or men who resembled them. It was a relief when he finally crossed the room and sat on the sofa.

She didn't dare take a seat on the sofa near him. Instead she went to the leather armchair nearest to the balcony, sat down and bent her head for just a moment. She wasn't sure she was praying for divine guidance, but some certainly wouldn't go amiss right now. When she lifted her gaze and met his again, she knew that the only defense she had was the truth.

"I am not marrying for love," she said baldly.

If she'd expected him to be shocked or to protest, she got her own shock at his reply.

He shrugged. "Love is highly overrated." His tone was harsh, almost bitter.

Now it was her turn to stare. This from the man whose wedding had been touted as the love match of the year? "But you—"

He cut her off abruptly. "This is not about me, remember?"

"No. You're right. I'm the one who—who suggested…*asked*," she corrected herself, needing to face her foolishness as squarely as she could. "I was just…remembering the girl I used to be." She studied her hands, then looked up again. "I was thinking about when I was in college and I had hopes and dreams and wonderful idealistic notions." She paused and leaned forward, needing him at least to understand that much. "Today when I saw you, I remembered that girl. And tonight, well, it was as if she was here again. As if I were her. You brought it all back to me!"

She felt like an idiot saying it, and frankly she expected him to laugh in her face. But he didn't. He didn't say anything at all for a long moment. His expression was completely inscrutable. And then he said slowly, almost carefully, "You were trying to find your idealistic youth?"

He didn't sound as if he thought she was foolish. He actually seemed intrigued.

Hesitantly, Anny nodded. "Yes. And then, when you said you'd do anything…" Her voice trailed off. It sounded unutterably foolish now, what she'd wanted. "I thought of those dreams and how they were gone. And I just…wanted to touch them one more time. Before—before…" She stopped, shrugging. "It sounds stupid now. I didn't mean to put you on the spot. But it was like some fairy tale—this night—and…" She felt her face warm again "I just wished—" She spread her hands helplessly.

He was the one who leaned forward now, resting his elbows just above his knees, his fingers loosely laced as he looked at her. "So why are you marrying him?"

"There are…reasons." She could explain them, but that would mean explaining who she was, and she'd ruined enough of her fairy-tale evening without destroying it completely. She didn't want Demetrios thinking of her as some spoiled princess who couldn't have her own way. For just one night she wanted to be a woman in her own right. Not her father's daughter. Not a princess.

Just Anny.

Even if she looked like an idiot, she'd be herself.

"Good reasons?"

She nodded slowly.

"But not love?" His tone twisted the word so that it still didn't sound as if he believed in it.

But Anny did.

"Maybe it will come," she said hopefully. "Maybe I haven't given him enough of a chance. He's quite a bit older than I am. A widower. His first wife died. He—he loved her."

"Better and better," Demetrios said grimly.

"That's another of the reasons I asked," she admitted. "I just thought that if I had this one night…with you…then if he never did love me, if it was always just a 'business arrangement' at least I'd…have had this. It's just one night. No strings. No obligations. I wasn't expecting anything else," she added, desperate to reassure him.

He was silent and again she had no idea what he was thinking. And he didn't tell her. There was nothing but silence between them.

Seconds. Minutes. Probably not aeons, but it felt that way. Millions of years of mortification. What had been a magical night had become, through her own fault, the worst night of her life.

Outside she heard the muffled sound of a car passing in the street below and, nearby, the ticking of Tante Isabelle's ornate French Empire brass-and-ebony mantel clock. Finally she heard him draw in a slow careful breath.

"All right, Anny Chamion," he said, getting to his feet and crossing the room to hold out his hand to her. "Let's do it."

She stared.

At his outstretched hand. Then her gaze slid up his arm to his broad chest, to his whisker-shadowed jaw, to that gorgeous mouth, to the memorable groove in his cheek, to those amazing green eyes, dark and slumberous now, and more compelling than ever. She swallowed.

"Unless you've changed your mind," he said when she didn't speak or even more. He looked at her, waiting patiently, and she knew he expected that she would have changed it.

But she couldn't.

Faced with a lifetime of duty, of responsibility, of a likely loveless marriage, she desperately needed something more. Something that would sustain her, make her remember the passion, the intensity, the joy she'd believed in as a girl.

She needed something to hang on to, her own secret.

And his.

She reached up and took Demetrios's hand. Then she stood and walked straight into his arms. "I haven't changed my mind."

When she slid into his embrace, Demetrios felt a shock run through him.

It was like the sudden bliss of diving into the water after a burning hot day.

It was pure and right and beautiful.

He could almost feel his body reawaken, as his eyes opened to Anny's upturned face as she lifted her lips to his.

He took what she offered. Gently at first. With a tentativeness that reminded him of his first fumbling teenage kisses. As if he'd forgotten how.

He knew he hadn't. He knew he'd been burned so badly by Lissa that he'd learned to equate kisses with betrayal.

But this wasn't Lissa. These lips weren't practiced.

These lips were as tentative as his own. Even more hesitant. Infinitely gentle. Sweet.

And Demetrios drank of their sweetness. He took his time, settling in, soaking up the sensations, remembering what it was like to kiss with hope, with joy, with something almost akin to innocence.

That was what they were giving each other tonight—a

reminder of who they had been. Not to each other, but as a young man and a young woman with dreams, ideals, hopes.

He didn't have hopes like those anymore. Lissa had well and truly ground those into the dust. But right now, kissing Anny, he could remember what it had felt like to be young, hopeful, aware of possibilities.

It was as powerful and intoxicating a feeling as any he could recall.

So why not enjoy it?

Why not celebrate the simple pleasure of one night with this woman who tasted of apple tart and sunshine, of citrus and red wine, and of something heady and slightly spicy—something Demetrios had never tasted before.

What was it? He wanted to know.

So he deepened the kiss, trying to discover more, trying to capture whatever was tantalizing him. He touched his tongue to hers and a second later felt the swirl of hers touching his.

At its touch his whole body responded with an urgency that surprised him. He might have deliberately forgotten these things, but his body hadn't.

It knew precisely what it wanted.

It wanted Anny. Now.

But as much as he was willing to take her to bed, he resisted his body's urgent demands to simply have his way with her right then and there.

Granted, this was going to be a one-off. But it wasn't a sleazy one-night stand, a quick mindless exercise in sexual gratification.

She wanted it for reasons of her own. And Demetrios, understanding them, decided she had a point. Yes, he was older and wiser now. But he could still appreciate the hopeful young man he'd once been. There was something satisfying about paying tribute to that man.

But it wasn't just about the past. It was about the present—the woman in his arms and making it beautiful for her as well. If he was going to be her memory, by God, he wanted to be a good one.

So he drew a deep breath and told himself to take his time as he let his hands slide slowly up her arms and over her back as he molded her to him.

She was warm and soft and womanly—and wearing far too many clothes. Demetrios couldn't ever remember seducing a woman who had been wearing so many clothes. Anny was still wearing her jacket, for heaven's sake.

Of course, he wasn't actually seducing her. He was enjoying what had been offered, and giving pleasure—and memories—in return.

In doing so, Demetrios discovered how much pleasure there was in removing all those clothes. First he eased her jacket off, slowly peeling it off her shoulders and down her arms, then tossed it aside. His fingers eased themselves beneath the hem of her silk top and brushed her even silkier skin.

He caressed it with his fingers as he kissed his way down to nuzzle her neck. He traced the line of her bra beneath, brushed his fingers over her nipples, and smiled at the quick intake of her breath and the way her fingers clutched at his back.

He drew back to share the smile with her. She stared up at him, her lips parted in a small O that made him bend his head and touch his lips to hers.

This time her tongue was there first, tasting, teasing. And he felt his body quicken in response. The last thing he wanted now was to go slow. He wanted to rip their clothes off and plunge into her as fast and furiously as he could.

He couldn't. He wouldn't. But he wanted to do more than kiss her. Soon.

"Have you got a bed somewhere, Anny Chamion?" he murmured against her lips.

She smiled as her tongue lingered against his lips for a second longer before she took his hand in hers. "Right this way."

In all her years as a princess Anny had never identified with Cinderella.

That made sense, of course, because Cindy hadn't been a princess in the beginning. She'd become one by taking a risk—

daring to do what she wasn't supposed to do—not for a happy ending, but for the joy of one single beautiful night.

And that Anny could identify with completely.

She, too, wanted a single beautiful night. A night that she could remember forever—a night that would get her through, not the endless drudgery of Cinderella's pre-prince future or even the endless succession of royal duties and obligations that were hers, but a passionless, loveless marriage.

Oh, she supposed there was a tiny chance that Gerard might come to love her the way he had loved Ofelia. But the instant Anny allowed its theoretical possibility, she knew that in truth it was never going to happen.

If Gerard had been going to fall in love with her, he would have done so before now. He'd had years, literally, to do it. As had she. It wasn't going to happen.

But Gerard had at least known love. Anny hadn't.

And she wanted to. Once. Just once. She wasn't asking for forever. Only for tonight—with Demetrios Savas.

Making love with him wouldn't be the deep abiding love that Gerard had shared with Ofelia. Anny knew that. Besides good conversation and dinner, she and Demetrios had shared nothing at all.

But she had memories of him that their meeting today brought back to life. Ever since he'd swept her out of the hotel this afternoon, she'd felt the same sort of heady enchantment she had known from the years when everything had seemed possible.

When he'd asked what on earth she was thinking, she had told him the truth. She wanted to recapture the young woman she'd been—just for this night—and give her a taste of the joy she'd longed for. And the young Demetrios she hadn't really known, but had only dreamed of, had been part of that young woman's life.

All she could think was that today, when he'd walked into the Ritz, kissed her and swept her out again, it was as if God or serendipity or fate or—who knew what?—had dropped him into her life for a reason.

This reason, she thought as she lay back on her bed and took hold of his hands and drew him down beside her.

That Anny wasn't a practiced lover was pretty much the understatement of the year. Her spine usually stiffened whenever Gerard slipped an arm around her or pressed a kiss to her cheek or lips. But now, when Demetrios kissed her, she felt as if she had no bones at all.

His lips were warm and firm and eager. And so were hers.

His had followed his fingers, kissing her shoulders, as he'd peeled off her jacket on the way to the bedroom. Now those same fingers slid beneath her silk top and his lips followed again, right up to the edge of her lacy bra.

He drew her top up and over her head with the skill of a man who knew exactly how to undress a woman. And for a brief moment Anny thought about all the beautiful women he must have known intimately—women far more practiced and appealing than she was.

And yet he didn't seem distracted by those memories. He was focused only on her. He made Anny feel as if she were the only woman in the world.

Demetrios's eyes, so green in the light, were dark now in the shadows. The skin seemed taut across his cheekbones. And Anny thought she felt a faint tremor in his fingers as they skimmed across her ribs, then pulled her up against him while he deftly unfastened her bra and drew it off.

He knelt on the bed beside her and pressed kisses along the line of her bare shoulders, then moved lower to her breasts, cupping them in his hands, and kissing them. The feel of his mouth on her heated flesh was more erotic than anything Anny had ever experienced. She clutched at his arms, hung on.

His hair tickled her nose as he nuzzled her. It smelled of the sea and of pine, and Anny drew a deep breath, as if she could capture the scent and save it forever. The memory would be more tangible that way.

And then he was kissing his way down the valley between her breasts all the way to her waistband. Only when his fingers sought the fastening, she caught her breath, then shook her head.

He pulled back, his brow furrowed, his hair tousled. "No?"

Anny wanted to smooth his brow. "Yes," she assured him.

"But…I don't want to be the only one undressed." She gave him a hopeful look, at the same time wondering if she was stepping out of bounds. She knew all the royal protocol in the world, and not a bit about whether she should be asking to take an active role in undressing the man she was in bed with. Maybe she should have been busy with his buttons already.

Demetrios's mouth quirked briefly and she wondered if he would tell her so, but he didn't. He just smiled and settled back on his heels, then dropped his hands to rest on his thighs. "Be my guest."

Anny swallowed. Then she levered herself up to sit against the headboard of the bed. She felt awkward as she reached out to touch him, but her hands didn't. They knew precisely what to do, taking hold of the buttons of his shirt, undoing them one by one, exposing his bare chest to her gaze.

And as she parted his shirt, the tips of her fingers brushed against the wiry curling hair that arrowed down from his chest to the waistband of his jeans.

Demetrios's jaw tightened as he watched her every move, breathing shallowly, his eyes hooded, his body totally still, as if he were steeling himself to endure some sort of pain.

"Are you all right?" she asked him worriedly.

He gave a hoarse laugh. "Oh, yeah. More than all right." Then abruptly he shrugged his shirt off, tossed it aside, took her hands and pressed them against his chest.

His skin was hot and damp and she could feel his heart thundering beneath her palm. Instinctively Anny leaned forward and touched her lips to his chest. Kissed him there, loved the feel of his heated flesh beneath her lips. She moved higher, kissed his collarbone, then his shoulders. She kissed his neck, nuzzled against his stubbled jawline, nibbled his ear, then traced it with her tongue and felt him shudder.

His response made her smile with a heady sense of power and excitement as she understood that he wanted her every bit as much as she wanted him.

And then he was bearing her back on the bed, where he made quick work of the zip on her linen trousers, hooked his thumbs in the waistband, skimmed them down her legs and dropped them onto the floor.

She should have felt self-conscious when he settled back to let his eyes roam over her. But all she felt was desire. And need.

Anny reached for his belt eagerly, but her hands weren't expert now and she fumbled with it.

Demetrios stilled her fingers. "Let me." He had it undone and was skinning out of his jeans in a matter of seconds. And then he was settling between her knees, running his hands up her thighs. Anny stroked his, too.

Demetrios tried to take it slow. He understood that she wasn't in the habit of propositioning men. Her touch was tentative, but no less tantalizing for being so.

The truth was that her unpracticed touch was more erotic than anything he'd felt in years. Of course, Lissa had been a skilled lover. But knowing she'd got her skills from sleeping with dozens of men was something he'd done his best to blot out of his mind.

Anny's touch was nothing like Lissa's. As her fingers skimmed over his body, he felt as if she were learning him and reawakening him at the same time.

It was almost like being reborn.

After the drama and trauma of his life with Lissa, he'd deliberately and determinedly shut off that part of himself. He'd refused to touch. Refused to feel.

Until tonight. Now, tonight, with her warm smiles, her gentle demeanor and soft touch, not to mention a certain artless allure that he doubted she was even aware of, Anny had unwittingly opened that door.

She made him feel again. Need again. Ache with desire in a way he hadn't since he was barely more than a boy. Both of them were connecting with their youthful selves tonight, Demetrios thought as he ran his hands over the line of her ribs, the slight swell of her hip, her long, lovely thigh to her knee, then slowly traced a line up the inside of that same thigh.

She quivered. So did he.

She lifted a hand and drew her fingers lightly down his

chest. Lower. And as she did, the heel of her hand brushed against his erection, a simple unintentional touch nearly sending him over the edge.

His breath hissed between his teeth. "Careful," he said, his voice shaky. "I'm a little overeager tonight. It's been a long time."

Her eyes widened. She looked stricken. "Oh! Oh, I'm sorry," she said, putting the meaning he hadn't said into the words he had. She started to sit up, to pull away. "I didn't mean—I should never have—"

But he caught her and held her right where she was. "It's fine," he assured her. "More than fine," he added truthfully. "I'm…looking forward to it."

And there was an understatement for you.

But Anny didn't look convinced. "I never thought—"

He shook his head. "Now's not the time to think."

He tugged her panties down her endless legs, then stripped his boxers off as well. Her gaze went at once to his erection. She swallowed, then reached out a hand to stroke him.

"Wait. Hang on." He was gritting his teeth as he reached down to snag his jeans and pull a condom packet from his wallet. With clumsy fingers he sheathed himself quickly, then settled between her thighs.

He wanted to simply dive in, to lose himself in her heat and her softness. But he knew better, knew that as much as he wanted this, really it was for her. And so he forced himself to slow down, to draw a line from her navel south, dipping his fingers between her thighs, watching as her eyes widened and her breath caught in her throat.

She was damp, ready. Her body moved restlessly as his fingers probed her. She bit her lip and her fingers knotted in the bed clothes. Her breaths were quick and shallow. His were, too. He was dying with need, but still he waited, touched. Stroked.

And then suddenly Anny ground her teeth and reached for him. "Yes! Now. I need—" The words caught in her throat. She tossed her head.

"What do you need?" Demetrios could barely get his own words past his lips. His voice was as strained an desperate as his body felt.

"Need…you!"

No more than he needed her. He'd reached the end of his endurance, and now he drove into her, felt her stiffen, heard her gasp.

His whole body froze. She couldn't be! Surely she wasn't a virgin! For God's sake! Why on earth would she have thrown her virginity away on one night with him?

It didn't make sense. He couldn't think. He could only feel. And want. Still. Then she shifted her body, accommodated him, settled against the mattress and dug her heels into his buttocks, driving him deeper.

He groaned. He had to be wrong. Of course he was wrong. But he tried to move slowly, carefully, to control his desperation.

But Anny's fingers gripped his shoulders. "It's all right," Anny said fiercely through her teeth. "It's all right," she said again when he still didn't move.

"You're sure? You're not— I thought you were—" But then she moved beneath him, her body seducing him, driving him insane, shattering the last of his control.

His world splintered as he buried himself inside her. He knew he had left her behind. He had failed.

"Oh!" There was a sudden delighted breathlessness in her voice that made Demetrios lift his head to stare at her.

"Oh?" he echoed warily.

Her face seemed to light up. "It was…wonderful." She was smiling at him. Even in the dim glow of the streetlamp beyond the window he could see her beaming. He didn't understand it at all.

"It wasn't wonderful," he told her abruptly.

Her smile vanished. "I'm sorry. I thought you…"

"I did. Obviously. And it was amazing for me," he assured her. "Absolutely." Mind-blowing in fact. "But that doesn't excuse my lack of control."

She smiled and touched a hand to his arm. "I…liked your…lack of control."

He stared at her. She liked it? He gave a quick disbelieving shake of his head. "I don't see why," he muttered.

"Because…because…" But she couldn't explain it. It was

simply enough to know that he'd wanted her, had lost himself in her. "You made me happy," she told him.

"Yeah?" He still couldn't quite fathom that. "I'll make you happier," he vowed.

And he set about doing just that.

If their first lovemaking had been short and, for him, desperate, this time Demetrios had considerably more finesse. More control. He kissed her thoroughly, taking his time, enjoying the soft sounds she made as he roused her desire. He let her slip the condom on him this time, and tried not to shudder with the desire her soft hands provoked.

She was perfect, fresh, beautiful, and responsive. And Demetrios was determined to give her the memories she'd asked him for.

As he made love to her he thought about the young woman she must have been then, and found himself wishing that he'd known her. At the same time he didn't imagine she'd changed much. There was an innocent sweetness about her even now. He didn't let himself think about the future she had predicted for herself. That was her choice—her life—not anything to do with him.

What he could do for her was what she'd asked—give her a night to remember.

He loved her completely, thoroughly, made her need his touch so that finally she clutched at his hips and drew him in.

"Yes." The word hissed through her teeth as she shattered around him. And as he brought her to climax, he understood her satisfaction at his own earlier loss of control.

It meant as much—even more—to give pleasure as to receive it, he thought even as his own climax overtook him and he buried himself in her body and felt himself wrapped in her arms.

Making love with Demetrios was everything Anny had ever dreamed of. More. It was as perfect as Cinderella's night at the ball.

She wanted to cry and at the same time she'd never felt happier—or more bereft—in her life because it was so wonderful and she knew it couldn't last.

Had always known, she reminded herself. Had gone into it with her eyes wide open. It was what she'd wanted, after all.

Memories.

Well, now she had them. In spades. She would remember this night always. Would savor it a thousand times. A million. All her life and the eternity that stretched beyond it. She would never forget.

Even now as she lay beneath Demetrios's sweat-slicked body and ran her still trembling hands down his smooth hard back, she focused on every single sensation, storing up the sound of his breathing, the weight of his body pressing on hers. She memorized the feel of his hair-roughened calves beneath her toes, the scent of the sea that seemed inexplicably so much a part of him, the scrape of his jaw against her cheek.

She catalogued them all, wishing she could create some tangible reminders to take out whenever she wanted to relive these moments. She was in no hurry at all to have him roll off her, create a space between them, smile down at her and say he had to go.

And when at last his breathing slowed and he rolled off, she felt an instant sense of loss. She wanted to clutch him back, to cling, to beg for more.

She didn't. He had given her what she asked for. He had given her the most memorable night of her life. Anny told herself not to be greedy, but to be grateful. And content.

"Thank you," she said quietly.

He seemed surprised. He raised up on one elbow and regarded her from beneath hooded lids. His mouth quirked at one corner. "I think I'm the one who should be saying thank you." For all that he smiled, his words were grave.

Still, they made her happy. She was glad he'd enjoyed their lovemaking. She didn't expect he would hang on to the memories forever as she would, but she hoped he might have occasional fleeting fond thoughts of this night—of her.

"You gave me wonderful memories," she assured him.

He opened his mouth, as if he might say something. But then he closed it again and simply nodded. "Good."

He didn't move. Neither did she. They stared at each other. Under Demetrios's gaze, for the first time Anny felt self-conscious. None of the royal protocol she'd ever learned—not even her year in the Swiss finishing school—had prepared her for the proper way to end this encounter.

Perhaps because it hadn't been proper in the least.

But she didn't regret it. She would never regret it.

"I should go," Demetrios said.

She didn't hang on to him. She stayed where she was in the bed, but she watched his every move as he dressed. This night was all she was going to have—she didn't want to so much as blink.

He didn't look at her or speak until he had finished dressing and was slipping on his shoes. Then his gaze lifted and his eyes met hers.

"You…should maybe rethink this marriage you're planning," he said.

She didn't answer. Didn't want to spoil the present by thinking about the future. Silently she got out of bed and wrapped herself in the dressing gown she'd left hanging over the chair. Then she crossed the room to him and took his hands in hers.

"Thank you," she said again, refusing to even acknowledge his comment. He opened his mouth as if he would say something else, then shut it firmly and shook his head. His gaze was steely as he met hers.

"It's your life," he said at last.

Anny nodded, made herself smile. "Yes."

She didn't say anything else. She needed him to go while she still had the composure she'd promised herself she would hang on to. It was only one night, she told herself.

It wasn't, she assured herself, as if she was in love with him.

That would teach him, Demetrios thought when he got back to his hotel. He flung himself over onto his back and stared at the hotel room ceiling. Though what he'd learned this evening he wasn't exactly sure.

Probably that women were the most confusing difficult contrary people on earth.

He should have known that already, having been married to Lissa. But Anny had seemed totally different. Sane, for one thing.

And yet all the while they'd been sitting there and he'd been thinking she was simply enjoying dinner and his company and having a good time she'd been thinking about inviting him into her bed.

It boggled the mind.

Still, when she explained, he'd understood. God knew sometimes over the past three years he'd yearned for the days when he'd believed all things were possible.

He didn't believe it anymore, of course. He wasn't looking for a relationship again. He'd done that with Lissa. He'd been the poster boy for idealism in those days—and look where it had got him.

No more. Never again.

From here on out he wanted nothing more than casual encounters. No hopes. No dreams. No promises of happily ever after.

Exactly what he'd had tonight with Anny.

Who was getting married, for God's sake! Talk about mind-boggling. But he supposed she was more of a realist than he had been. Though why the hell a beautiful, intelligent young woman was marrying some elderly widower was beyond him.

And why was the elderly widower marrying her?

Stupid question. Why wouldn't any man—who still believed in marriage—want to marry a bright fresh beautiful woman like Anny?

But if he had been the marrying kind and engaged to her, Demetrios knew damned well he wouldn't leave her feeling luke-warm and desperate enough to invite another man into her bed!

He was sure she didn't do that very often. Or ever.

For a minute there, when he'd entered her, he'd thought she was a virgin. But that didn't make sense.

He wished he knew what was going on.

Was her family destitute? Did they owe money to this man? Was Anny being bartered for their debts?

It certainly didn't look as if they had money worries from the apartment she was living in. Of course she'd told him at dinner that she was staying in the flat of her late mother's best friend, Anny's own godmother, a woman she called Tante Isabelle. While Isabelle was in Hong Kong doing something for a bank, she'd lent Anny her apartment for the year.

So why wasn't Tante Isabelle, who obviously cared enough for Anny to provide her a place to live, objecting to her god-daughter's loveless marriage?

Did she even know it was a loveless marriage?

Where was Anny's father? He was still living, Demetrios knew that. Anny had mentioned him in the present tense. He was married again. She'd mentioned a stepmother and three little stepbrothers.

Was she doing it for them?

Whatever the "good reasons" were, she didn't seem to be doing it for herself. So who was she doing it for? And why?

Stop it! he commanded himself roughly. It wasn't his problem. *She* wasn't his problem.

He'd done his part. He'd taken her to bed. He'd made love with her and had, presumably, reminded her of the idealistic girl she'd been. He'd given her the memories she wanted.

He had a few himself. Not that he intended to bring them out and remember them. And yet, when he attempted to shut them away, they wouldn't go. He could still see her in his mind's eye—bright-eyed and laughing, gentle and serene, eager and responsive.

They were far better memories than those he had of Lissa.

They should have relaxed him, settled him. His body was sated. It was his mind that wouldn't stop replaying the evening.

He tossed and turned until eventually the bed couldn't confine his restlessness. He got up to prowl the room, to open the floor-to-ceiling window that opened overlooking La Croisette and the sea.

To the west he could see the shape of the Palais du Festival beyond the boulevard. Past that was the harbor where Theo was on his sailboat. Beyond that the hill and buildings of Le Soquet rose against the still dark sky.

Anny was there.

He could be, too, he thought. He was sure she would have let him stay the night.

But he didn't want to stay the night, he reminded himself. He wanted brief encounters. No involvement. He shoved away from the window and shut it firmly.

He wasn't going to care about any woman ever again. Not even sunny, smiling Anny Chamion with her upcoming loveless marriage, her hidden dreams and her memories of the lovemaking they'd shared.

It was going on five. He had a breakfast meeting at eight with Rollo Mikkelsen, who was in charge of distribution for Starlight Studios. He needed to be sharp. He needed to have his wits about him. He didn't need to be thinking about Anny Chamion.

He yanked on a pair of running shorts and tugged a T-shirt over his head. Maybe running a few miles could do what nothing else had done.

He pocketed his room key and went downstairs into the cool Cannes morning. He crossed La Croisette and bounced on his toes a few times, then he set out at a light jog. The pavement was nearly deserted still. In a couple of hours it would start to get busy. The day would begin.

He would meet with Rollo. There would be more meetings after that. Lunch with a producer he hoped to work with down the road. And late this afternoon the screening.

Afterward he'd go see Franck. He was tempted to see if Franck wanted to come to the screening, but it wasn't an action hero story. It was a dark piece—the only sort of thing he had been capable of writing in the aftermath of his marriage and circumstances of Lissa's death. It was a cautionary tale.

Not exactly fodder for a teenager who still had his life ahead of him. No. Better that he go see Franck after.

Would Anny be there?

It didn't matter if she was.

Demetrios picked up his pace, refusing to let himself think about that. He didn't care. They'd had one evening. One night of loving. One night in which they'd each recaptured a part of the young idealistic people they'd once been.

They'd given that to each other. But now it was over.

Time to move on.

CHAPTER FOUR

ANNY DIDN'T SEE Demetrios again.

She didn't really expect she would.

But as she went about her business, as she walked to the clinic, did her grocery shopping, worked on her dissertation, and actually went to a screening or two at the Palais du Festival over the next ten days, she couldn't help keeping an eye out to see if she could spot the tall dark-haired man who had so startlingly swept into her life.

He had gone back to the clinic. She knew that because Franck had been full of the information. And he hadn't only come the next day as he'd promised, but also several times over the past week and a half.

Yesterday, Franck had told her gleefully this afternoon, he had commandeered a wheelchair and taken Franck down to the dock.

"A wheelchair? You went to the dock?" Anny, who had never been able to get Franck to go anywhere because he was too self-conscious, could barely believe her ears. "Whatever for?"

"We went sailing."

Then she really did gape.

Franck nodded eagerly. "We went in his brother's sailboat."

He recounted his amazing day, his eyes shining as he told her how Demetrios and his brother Theo—"a racing sailor," Franck reported—had simply lifted him out of the wheelchair and into the boat, then set out for a sail around the Îles de Lérins.

Anny was still stuck imagining Franck allowing himself to

be lifted, but apparently, as far as Franck was concerned, Demetrios and his brother could do anything. "Didn't he tell you?" Franck demanded.

Anny shook her head. "I haven't seen him."

He looked surprised. "You should have come in the mornings. He always came then."

Of course he did. Because he knew when she went to see Franck. She'd told him. If Demetrios had wanted to see her, he could have. He knew where she lived.

He hadn't. And she hadn't sought him out, either.

She'd had her night. She'd relived it ever since.

Of course she couldn't deny having wished it had lasted longer—even wishing it had had a future. But she knew it didn't.

So it was better that she not encounter him again. So even though she had kept an eye out for him over the following week and a half, she'd carefully avoided attending any parties to which he might have gone.

Of course, she knew he'd come to Cannes to work, not to party. But she also knew that sometimes going to parties *was* part of the work. Some years it had even been part of her own. Fortunately her father had decided not to host one this year.

And now the festival was over. Demetrios, she was sure, was already gone. He'd got what he came for. News stories early this week had reported that he'd landed a big distributor for the film he'd brought to Cannes. And yesterday she'd read that he'd found backing for his next project.

She was happy for him. She almost wished she had seen him again to tell him so. But what good would that have done, really?

It would only have been embarrassing. He might even have believed she was stalking him.

No. She'd already had her own personal fairy tale with Demetrios Savas. One night of lovemaking.

That was enough.

But when Gerard had called her that afternoon and announced, "We will be hosting a party on the royal yacht this evening," she wasn't quite as sanguine as she'd hoped.

She'd told herself that she would go to her fate gracefully and willingly. He was a good man. A kind man.

But the truth was, she'd barely given him a thought since the night she'd had dinner with Demetrios.

Now she felt oddly cold and disconnected as she repeated, "We?" Did he meant the royal "we" or "the two of them"?

"My government," Gerard clarified briskly. "The party was planned to occur whether I was here or not. We hoped to attract film companies, you know. The revenues are an excellent boost to the economy."

"Yes, of course." Her father believed that, too.

"And since I've finished my work in Toronto, I'm able to be here. And it will be a wonderful opportunity for us to host it together." He sounded delighted.

Anny wasn't certain. "Are you sure I should host it with you?" she asked. "I mean, we're not married." As if he needed reminding.

"Not yet," Gerard agreed. "But soon. That is something we need to discuss, Adriana."

"What is?"

"The date of our wedding."

"I thought we agreed we'd wait until after I finished my doctorate."

"Yes, but we can make plans. It will not be an elopement, you know."

"Of course not. But there will be time—"

"Yes," Gerard said cheerfully. "Tonight. After the party."

"But—"

"So, no, you will not be my official hostess," he went on, "but we have waited long enough. I've missed you, Adriana."

"I've—" Anny swallowed "—missed you, too."

He heard the hesitation in her voice. "You are upset that I wasn't here last week."

"No. I—"

"I'm sorry I couldn't be," he explained to her. "Duty called. It often does," he added wryly. "You understand. Better than anyone, you understand."

"Yes."

"But I am here now. And I'm looking forward to seeing you tonight. I will be there for you at eight." He rang off before she could object.

Object? Hardly. Gerard had the same ability to command that her father did. It came from a lifetime of expecting people to fall in with his plans. And even if he had stayed on the phone, what possible objection could she have made?

Of course he had sprung it on her at the last minute. But it wasn't as if she couldn't pull herself together, find a dress, be prepared to leave at eight.

Princesses were always prepared. It was part of their job description.

She just wished she felt more prepared to marry him.

"His Highness regrets that he is unable to come in person," the driver said respectfully as he bowed, then helped Anny into the back of the black sedan that had arrived outside her flat at precisely 8:00 p.m. "He is hosting a dinner meeting. He will be on the yacht when you arrive."

Anny tried to look regretful, too. But what she felt was relief. While she could make conversation with anyone anywhere, thinking about being alone with Gerard in the confines of the car had made her edgy for the past three hours.

He would be all that was proper and polite. And so would she. They would make small talk. Discuss the weather. His trip to Toronto. Her latest chapter notes on her dissertation.

Or their upcoming wedding.

She flashed a quick smile at the driver. "*C'est bien. Merci.*"

He shut the door, and immediately the silence enveloped her. Sometimes riding in cars like this suffocated her. She felt as if she were buffered from the real world, isolated, with the sounds and commotion beyond the doors held firmly at bay.

But right now, for a few minutes, she welcomed it. The short ride to the harbor would give her a chance to compose her thoughts, to prepare herself, to become the princess of Mont Chamion she would have to be this evening.

But as the car approached the harbor, she became distracted by the rows of yachts and sailboats, thinking about how Demetrios and his brother had brought Franck here. Now she scanned the multitude of boats as if, just by looking, she might be able to tell which one was Theo's.

Of course chances were very good Demetrios's brother was already gone. And it didn't matter anyway. The memories of her night with Demetrios had been intended for her to take out and savor, yes. But they weren't intended to distract her from the obligations at hand.

Now, though, even when she turned her gaze away from the harbor and stared resolutely straight ahead, it wasn't the driver she saw. In her mind's eye she still saw Demetrios making love with her.

"Go away," she muttered under her breath.

The driver glanced around at the sound of her voice and met her gaze in the rearview mirror. "I beg your pardon, Your Highness?"

"Nothing." Anny pressed her fingers to her temples, feeling a heachache coming on. "I was simply thinking aloud."

And she needed to stop. Now.

A small launch carried her to where the royal yacht lay at anchor. As they approached the yacht she could see tuxedo-clad staff scurrying around. She caught snatches of the lively sounds of live music. Maybe she and Gerard would dance. He would hold her in his arms and they would find love together. It had happened that way for Papa and Mama. Her father had assured her it was so. Their marriage had been arranged and it had been wonderful. It could happen.

Determinedly Anny lifted her chin and made herself smile at the prospect.

She even made a point of minding her royal manners and staying primly seated until the crew brought the launch alongside the yacht when she would have preferred to stand up and let the wind whip through her hair or, worse yet, be the one to throw the line and clamber aboard the way she always had on her father's smaller yacht when she was a child.

So she was definitely in princess mode when she heard Gerard say, "Ah, wonderful. Here you are at last."

He was waiting on deck and gave her his hand to help her aboard, then let his gaze travel in slow admiration down the length of her navy blue dress with its galaxies of scattered silver sequins for a long moment before he kissed her on both cheeks.

Then, to her surprise, he wrapped her in a gentle embrace. "It's so good to see you again, my dear."

He truly did look pleased.

He was a lovely man, Anny reminded herself guiltily. Kind. Gentle. Capable of love. He had after all, by all accounts, loved his first wife very very much.

"Gerard," she greeted him warmly, and smiled not only with her lips but her voice as well.

He linked his arm through hers and drew her onto the deck beside him. "I'm so sorry I wasn't able to come and get you in person. But I had a dinner meeting with Rollo Mikkelsen. Come. I want you to meet him. Rollo is the head of Starlight Studios. He's interested in possibly setting future projects in Val de Comesque."

Anny smiled. "What wonderful news."

"It is." Gerard opened the door to the main salon where a table had been set for perhaps ten people. The meal was over now and the dinner guests had left the table to chat in small groups. "Rollo." He drew Anny with him toward the nearest group of men. "I'd like you to meet my fiancée."

They all turned as Gerard slipped an arm around Anny's waist and said proudly, "Her Royal Highness, Princess Adriana of Mont Chamion, may I present Rollo Mikkelsen, head of Starlight Studios."

A man took her hand.

Anny didn't see him at all. He was nothing but a blur. Her heart pounded. She smiled perfunctorily, murmured politely, "Mr. Mikkelsen, a pleasure."

"And Daniel Guzman Alonso, the producer," Gerard said, introducing the next man.

Another blur. Another hand shook hers. Now her ears were ringing as well. Her voice worked, though, thank God. "Mr. Guzman Alonso, I'm delighted to meet you." Years of social deportment practice had something to recommend it, after all.

"And of course you must recognize Demetrios Savas," Gerard was saying jovially, "whose latest film Rollo has just agreed to distribute."

Demetrios was not a blur at all. Sharp and clear, tall and imposing. And, judging from the hard jade glare in those amazing eyes, somewhere between stunned and furious. His gaze raked her accusingly.

Anny could barely breathe. Nor could she stop her own eyes from fastening on him, hungrily, devouring him. Wanting him again so badly that how she could ever have thought one night would be enough, she hadn't a clue.

"Mr. Savas." She held out her hand to him, polite, proper, sounding—she hoped—perfectly composed.

Demetrios crushed it in his. "Your Highness," he said through his teeth. "Imagine meeting you here."

A princess?

Anny Chamion was a *princess*?

She was the "delightful fiancée Princess Adriana" that Gerard had mentioned over dinner?

His fiancée would be joining them later, the crown prince of Val de Comesque had said. She was busy with her day job—unspecified—and since he hadn't given her any warning, he'd only asked her to come to the party, not appear for dinner.

"Even we royals have to work hard these days," he'd joked. "You will meet her tonight."

Now here she was, with Gerard's arm around her, looking serene and elegant and every bit as royal as the man she was marrying.

Which made Gerard her "elderly widower"?

Demetrios's teeth came together with a snap. Maybe she hadn't used the term "elderly," but that was what he'd thought.

The slim fingers he was crushing between his were trying unsuccessfully to ease out of his grasp. For a moment he didn't even realize he was still gripping them.

Then, still staring into Anny's—no, *Princess* Adriana's—wide eyes, he dropped them abruptly, took a step back and shoved his hands into his pockets.

It was probably some sort of social solecism, to have his hands in his pockets in front of a princess, but short of strangling her, he could think of nothing else to do with them.

Besides, as far as social gaffes went, it was no doubt a bigger one to have slept with her!

He shot her a glare. He doubted she noticed. She wasn't looking at him. She was smiling at Rollo Mikkelsen, answering a question he'd asked her, her voice low and melodious, steady and completely at ease—just as if she were not standing between the man she was going to marry and the man she'd taken to her bed!

And he'd thought Lissa was a lying cheat!

Abruptly he said, "Excuse me. I see someone I need to speak to." And he turned and walked out of the room as fast as he could.

It was no bigger lie than hers. And almost at once he did see someone he knew. Mona Tremayne was standing on deck by herself, looking at the sunset, and even if it meant listening to her extol the virtues of her darling starlet daughter Rhiannon, he was determined to do it.

It was better than standing there listening to the lying *Princess* Adriana charm all and sundry while her fiancé looked on!

Mona was delighted to see him. She kissed him on both cheeks, then patted his arm. "It's lovely to see you, dear boy. I'm glad you're back among the living."

Demetrios took a careful breath and tried to focus solely on her. "It wasn't that bad," he told her. He liked Mona, always had. She called a spade a spade, and she couldn't help it if her daughter was a ditz.

"Maybe not for you. But we can't afford to let talent go to waste," she said with a throaty laugh caused by too many years of cigarettes. "You do good work. You've been missed."

"Thanks." His heart was still pounding, but he refused to look back toward the salon. He didn't gave a damn where the princess was. He slanted Mona a grin. "Does that mean I can toss an idea at you?"

"You want to marry my daughter?" Another wonderful husky Mona Tremayne laugh.

Demetrios managed a laugh of his own as he shook his head, "I'm through with marriage, Mona." Truer words had never been spoken.

"I'm not surprised," Mona said briskly, her eyes telling him that she knew more than he had said. Then she smiled and added, "Well, if you ever change your mind, you've got a fan in my household. More than one."

Demetrios smiled, too. "Thanks."

She leaned against the railing and stared out across the water before slanting him a sideways glance. "So toss me the idea," she suggested. "I'm listening."

It was the sort of chance he'd been waiting for all week. Mona at his disposal, her daughter nowhere to be found. And he did have an idea for her. He tried to pitch it.

He'd have done better if, a few minutes later, he hadn't been instantly distracted by the sound of Anny's voice nearby and the knowledge that she and Gerard had come out onto the deck.

He lost his train of thought as he glanced over his shoulder to see where she was. His fingers strangled the railing because he still wanted to grab her and shake her and demand to know why the hell she hadn't bothered to tell him who she really was. Not to mention what she thought she'd been doing inviting him into her bed!

He was still steaming. Still furious.

And not paying any attention at all to whatever Mona was saying in reply to his movie pitch.

"—think I'll jump overboard," Mona ended conversationally and looked at him brightly.

In the silence Demetrios recollected himself and tried to get a grip. "Huh?"

"Oh, my dear." Mona patted his cheek. "We should talk another time—when you can focus."

"I'm focusing," he insisted.

But only, it seemed, on Anny. He couldn't seem to make sense of anything beyond her soft voice somewhere behind him, followed by the melodious sound of her laughter. Then he heard Gerard, too, chiming in, speaking rapidly in French to whoever they were talking to, and then Anny switched to French as well. Their conversation went too quickly for him to have any idea what they were saying.

She sounded happy, though. Was she happy? What about her loveless marriage?

"But if I drowned, I couldn't be in your film then, could I?" Mona was saying.

He stared at her blankly.

She laughed, again. "Never mind, dear." She gave him air kisses and began to move away. "Another time. I think I'll find another drink."

"I'll get you a drink," he said hastily.

"No, dear boy. I'm fine. You stay here and entertain royalty." And giving his cheek one more pat, she swept away.

He turned to protest again—and came face-to-face with Anny.

Her wide eyes were searching his face. Her smile, so polished earlier, looked slightly more strained now. "Demetrios."

He drew himself up straight. "Your Highness," he said stiffly.

"Anny," she corrected, her voice soft, the way it had been in bed.

He ground his teeth. "I don't think so." His voice was, he hoped, pure steel. He braced his back and elbows against the railing, and glared down at her.

"Anny," she insisted. "It's who I am."

"Certainly not all of who you are," he reminded her sharply. "You could have told me." He looked around for Gerard, expecting him to appear at her side. But her prince had moved away and on the other side of the deck, deep in conversation with Rollo and another studio executive Demetrios knew.

"I could have," she admitted. "I didn't want to. Why should I?" Her tone was indifferent, as if it could make her idiocy appear perfectly reasonable.

"Because I might have liked to know?" he snapped.

No one was close to them. The sextet had begun to play. A clarinet was warbling. Thank God, because this wasn't a conversation anyone should be overhearing.

"I asked you to tell me what I should know about you," he reminded her.

"You didn't need to know that."

"You asked me to sleep with you!"

Color flared in her cheeks. She glanced around quickly as if fearing people would hear.

A corner of his mouth twisted. "Something else you don't want anyone to know? Afraid your elderly widower will learn what you were up to?"

"My what?" She looked confused.

"Your fiancé," he bit out. "The man who is oh-so old and decrepit and who doesn't love you."

"I never said he was elderly or decrepit. Gerard is twenty-one years older than I am," she said through her teeth. "Which may not seem like much to you, but it is a different generation."

He grunted, acknowledging that. But it didn't explain the rest. "So why are you marrying him? Daddy forcing you? Are you making a governmental alliance?" He spat the words.

"Something like that."

He snorted. "Give me a break. This is the twenty-first century!"

"It can still happen," she maintained.

"You're saying your old man sold you off to the highest bidder?"

"Of course not! It was simply…arranged. It's good for both countries."

"Countries? That's what matters? Not people?"

She lifted her chin. "Gerard is a fine man."

"Whom you betrayed by sleeping with me," he pointed out sardonically.

She opened her mouth as if she would deny it, but then she

closed it again, her lips pressing into a thin line. The color was high in her cheeks. She looked indignant, furious, and incredibly beautiful.

"Obviously I made a mistake," she said tightly, hugging her arms across her chest. "I was out of line. I never should have suggested anything of the sort. It was…" She stopped, her voice not so much trailing off as dropping abruptly.

"What was it?" Demetrios asked her, trying to fathom what was going on in that beautiful head of hers.

She shook it. "Nothing. Never mind. Forget it."

"Will you?" he asked her.

"Yes." The word came out quickly. Then her gaze dropped. So did her voice. "No."

At her soft yet stark admission, his own eyes jerked up to search her face, to try to understand her. Once he'd caught on to Lissa's duplicitous behavior, he began to have an inkling what she was up to, though God knew he'd had no idea how far she would go.

But Anny didn't sound like she was lying now. Not this time.

"Did it solve anything?" he pressed her.

She didn't answer. Finally, when he thought she wasn't going to reply at all, she shrugged. "I don't know." She wasn't looking at him now. She'd come to stand next to the railing, too, and now stared across the water toward the lights of Cannes. Her shoulders were slumped.

Demetrios was still angry, though whether he was more annoyed at her or at himself, he couldn't have said. After Lissa, he damned well should have known better. And what the hell was Anny doing, letting herself be a pawn?

It was none of his business, he reminded himself. He should turn and walk away. But his feet didn't take the hint. They stayed right where they were. Behind them the sextet had segued into something lilting and jazzy.

Anny didn't seem to notice. Her gaze never wavered from the shore.

"Fascinating, is it?" he demanded when she still didn't look at him.

"It's beautiful," she replied simply.

He grunted. "All lit up like a fairy tale," he said mockingly, keeping his eyes straight ahead.

"Some would say that," she agreed quietly.

"Not you?" He pressed her. The breeze lifted her hair. It smelled of citrus and the sea. He wanted to touch it, to brush it away from her face, hook it behind her ear, touch her cheek. Touch her.

He knotted his fingers together instead.

"I'm not a big believer in fairy tales," she said in a soft monotone.

"Except for one night," he reminded her harshly.

"I'm sorry. You could have said no," she pointed out.

His jaw tightened. "Should have said no," he corrected.

The breeze caught her hair again and tossed tendrils of it against his cheek. More citrus scent assailed his nostrils. Demetrios turned his head away, but just as quickly turned back to breathe in the scent again, to feel the softness touch his face.

She took a careful breath. "I want to thank you for going back to see Franck."

"No thanks necessary. I didn't do it for you," he said flatly.

"I know that. But even so, it means a great deal. To him," she added. "And taking him sailing." She turned her head to smile at him. "Brilliant. I can't believe you got him to do it. But he loved every minute."

Demetrios didn't want her thanks. He didn't want her smiles. He shrugged irritably. "I was glad to do it. He's a good kid. Smart. He's got a lot of potential."

"Yes." Anny smiled slightly. "I agree. I'm afraid he doesn't."

"He's angry. Given what happened to him, why shouldn't he be?" Demetrios remembered all the times in the past three years when his own anger had stopped him cold, threatening to derail his dreams. There were too many to count. Now he took a slow careful breath. "He'll find his way," he said. They continued to stare at the seafront in silence for a long moment, then he added, "He'll get there with some support from friends like you."

"And you," Anny added.

Demetrios shook his head. "I'm leaving. Bright and early tomorrow morning. I'm taking my brother's boat to Santorini."

"But you won't forget Franck." She sounded certain.

How could she know him well enough to be sure of that when he felt like she didn't know him at all? Demetrios didn't know. But he had to admit she was right in this case. "No, I won't forget him. I'll stay in touch."

She smiled, satisfied. "He'll like that." She stared down at the water, unspeaking for a long moment, but she didn't walk away.

Neither did he. He didn't feel as angry now. He couldn't have said why, except that this Anny, princess or not, was the one he remembered.

She brushed a lock of hair away from her face. "I thought you'd be gone by now. You got what you came for—excellent distribution, a highly acclaimed film."

"Rollo's taking it on, yes. And the critics have been kind."

"I'm sure it's not just kindness."

"You didn't see it?" Surely princesses could see whatever they wanted. Royal prerogative or some such thing.

"No. I—I wanted to. But I didn't want you to think—" She stopped.

"Think what?" he demanded.

She shrugged awkwardly. "That I was…chasing you. I meant what I said, one night. I told you the truth, Demetrios. I just…didn't tell you all of it." She had turned and was looking at him intently now, as if she were begging him to believe her.

Did he? Or was she as good an actress as Lissa?

It didn't matter, he reminded himself. Princess or not, she wasn't part of his life. Not after tonight.

But he couldn't stop himself saying, "Look, Anny. You can't do this if you're not sure. Gerard might be a great guy. But marriage is—" He let out a harsh breath, knowing he was the last person on earth who should be offering advice on marriage. But then, who knew better the mistakes you could make even when you thought you were marrying for love?

"Marriage is what?" she asked when he didn't go on.

"Marriage is too damned hard to risk on flimsy hopes!" He blurted the words angrily, not at her, but at Lissa.

Of course Anny didn't know that. She stared at him, eyes wide at his outburst.

Demetrios stared back. It was none of his business. *None of his business.* The words echoed over and over in his head.

"Adriana!" Gerard's voice behind them made them both start.

"I have to go," Anny said quickly.

Demetrios straightened up at once, and gave her a polite distant nod. "Of course."

But still she didn't move away. She faced him and looked into his eyes for a long moment, a slight smile on her face. "Thank you."

He raised a brow. "For the memories?" he said sardonically.

She nodded. Their gazes locked.

"Adriana!" Gerard's voice came again, more insistent this time.

Anny turned to go. Demetrios caught her hand and held her until she looked back at him. "Don't regret your life, princess."

Demetrios kept away from her the rest of the evening.

Of course he did. Why wouldn't he? He thought she'd used him and lied by omission. It hadn't felt like a lie. It had felt like being able—for once—to share herself, the woman, not the princess, that she really was.

But she didn't suppose Demetrios saw it that way. He was probably avoiding her. Or maybe he had forgotten her already. She was the one who had vowed to remember. And dear God, she was. Every single second Anny knew exactly where he was. She saw who he talked to, who talked to him.

As Gerard's unofficial hostess she was required to focus on other things, on all his guests. And no one could have faulted her attention to her role. She chatted with his guests, gave them what she hoped appeared to be her undivided attention—even when it was being shared with the tall, lean man with wind-blown hair talking to this producer or that actress.

Gerard kept her close, smiling at her and nodding his approval. "Your papa is right. You are marvelous," he told her.

Yes, Papa would be proud. But Anny's heart wasn't in it. Her soul wasn't in it. Only later that evening when, shortly before midnight, she saw Demetrios board the launch back to the harbor, did her heart and soul let her know where they were. A hollow desperate ache opened up inside her.

He wasn't for her. She knew that.

She repeated it over and over in her head even as she continued smiling brightly at the couple telling her about their South Pacific cruise. She nodded, commented, laughed at a witty remark and didn't miss a beat.

But she didn't miss the sight of Demetrios standing alone on the deck of the launch looking back at the yacht, either.

As soon as she could, she made her excuses and slipped away to stand in the bow of the royal yacht to catch a last glimpse of the launch as it grew smaller and smaller and finally merged with the lights of the harbor, and he was gone.

They were ships that passed in the night, she told herself. One night.

"Adriana!" Gerard's voice called to her once more.

She swallowed, then called, "*Je viens*. I'm coming."

She heard Demetrios's words echo in her mind. *Don't regret your life, princess.*

She prayed desperately that she wouldn't.

CHAPTER FIVE

DEMETRIOS WAS up at dawn.

He wanted an early start. He hadn't slept well. Not true. He hadn't slept at all. He'd gone to bed determined not to spare a thought for Her Royal Highness Princess Adriana.

And he couldn't get her out of his mind.

Of all the irritating demanding things that he'd anticipated having to cope with during these past two weeks in Cannes, dealing with a princess—or any woman at all, for that matter—had never made the list.

After Lissa, he couldn't imagine one breaching his defenses.

He'd allowed himself the one night with Anny because it had been clearly *one night*. No strings. No obligations. No relationship.

It still wasn't, he tried to tell himself. But until last night he'd managed to convince himself that she'd known what she was doing.

Now he didn't believe it for a minute. And he couldn't get her out of his head!

Fine, he'd get an early start. The sooner he set sail, the sooner he'd put Cannes—and Her Royal Highness—behind him.

He flung the last of his clothes into his bag and checked out of the small hotel where he'd spent the past two weeks. Then, hefting his duffel bag, he headed for the harbor. The morning was still and quiet, almost soundless so far. Few cars moved through the streets. A lone cyclist rode past him.

When he crossed La Croisette, there was a bit of traffic, a few pedestrians walked briskly on morning constitutionals, a couple of joggers ran by and he saw a man walking a dog. Cannes getting back to normal.

Demetrios wanted to get back to normal, too. He quickened his pace, eager to board the boat and be at sea at last.

Near the Palais du Festival, work crews were beginning to gather to take down the hospitality tents. He skirted them, heading for the dock where Theo had left his sailboat.

It was a magnificent boat—a bit over forty feet, sleek and trim, with two small cabin spaces fore and aft, and a main cabin that could sleep an extra kid or two if required. It was fast and fun and yet it could still accommodate Theo's new lifestyle as a married man with kids. He and Martha had two now—Edward, who was five, and Caroline, not quite three.

Demetrios had always figured himself for the family man, while Theo would always be the family's nautical equivalent of the Lone Ranger. That wasn't the way it had turned out.

"Lucky you," Demetrios had said, feeling a small stab of envy at Theo's life.

"Yeah." Theo hadn't misunderstood. "I hate taking the time to sail to Santorini with Martha and the kids there already. From here by myself it'll take me almost two weeks."

"Tell them to come here. Make a holiday of it."

Theo shook his head. "Caro's getting over croup. Martha worries. She's got commissions to work on. And Eddie gets seasick."

"Your son gets seasick?" Demetrios's mind boggled.

"He'll grow out of it. But we hate seeing him miserable. It isn't fun. And you know how it can blow this time of year."

They both had experienced their share of gale-force winds in the Mediterranean during frequent visits to Greece to see their mother's parents when they were children. "It's worse other times," he said truthfully.

Theo shrugged. "Fine. You do it."

Demetrios had thought he was joking.

"Never been more serious in my life. You want to sail her to Santorini after the festival, she's all yours."

Demetrios hadn't hesitated. "You bet."

The last time he'd sailed any great distance, it had been not long after his wedding. He'd chartered a sailboat so he and Lissa could sail from Los Angeles to Cabo.

"It'll be fantastic," he'd promised Lissa.

It had been a disaster—one of many in their short marriage.

But this trip wouldn't be. It wouldn't be a piece of cake to do it solo, but he had plenty of experience and, after Cannes, a real desire to be on his own. It was the carrot he'd held out for himself for the past two weeks, every time the festival threatened to drive him crazy.

Now he reached the dock and could spot Theo's boat tied up in a slip at the far end. A couple of men from the crew of one of the nearer yachts were already making ready to sail. They gave him a wave as he passed. He waved back, but kept moving,

The red-orange rays of sunrise were turning the gleaming hulls bright pink against still cerulean water. It looked like a painting.

Until someone stood up and moved away from where they had been sitting on the stern of the boat.

Demetrios stopped dead, disbelieving his eyes. He frowned, gave his head a shake, then came closer to be sure.

And she—he could tell it was a female, could even tell *which* female—came toward him, too. Even though she looked totally different.

Gone was the midnight blue dress that glittered like starlight when she moved. Gone were the diamond necklace and dangling diamond earrings. Gone was the sophisticated upswept hairstyle with its few escaping tendrils. There wasn't a hint of Princess Adriana in evidence anywhere.

Nor was there a hint of the classy competent professional woman he'd met that day at the Carlton. No blazer, no linen skirt, no casual dress shoes.

This Anny was wearing jeans and running shoes, a light-colored T-shirt with a sweatshirt knotted around her hips. And her hair was pulled back in a ponytail. Tendrils still escaped, but they made her look about fifteen.

Hell's bells, he thought. All the roles she played, she could give Lissa a run for her money!

"What are you doing here?" He was equal parts suspicion and annoyance. He was tempted to just brush right past.

"I came to say thank you."

His gaze narrowed. "For what? Sleeping with you? My pleasure." He made sure it didn't sound like it. "But don't come around thinking it's going to happen again."

"I know that," she said, with as much impatience in her voice as he had in his. "I didn't come for that."

"What then?

She hesitated a split second, then looked right up into his eyes. "For courage."

Demetrios didn't like the sound of that. He gave her a short, hard look, grunted what he hoped was a sort of "that's nice, now go away" sound. Then he did brush past her, tossing his duffel bag onto the deck and jumping on after it.

He heard her feet land on the deck barely a second after his. He spun around and confronted her squarely, stopping her in her tracks. "What do you think you're doing?"

"Telling you what happened."

He scowled at her. He supposed it was useless telling her he didn't want to know what happened. He folded his arms across his chest and leaned back against the rail. "So tell me."

"I…talked to Gerard last night. After the party. I told him I couldn't marry him."

Demetrios stared at her, aghast. Of course he'd seen her turmoil. But that didn't mean she needed to burn her bridges!

"Why?" he demanded harshly, suspiciously.

At his tone, her eyes widened. "You know why! Because I don't love him. Because he doesn't love me."

"So? You knew that last week. Hell, you probably knew it last year! Didn't stop you then."

"I know, but—"

But Demetrios didn't want to hear. He spun away, grabbing his duffel and tossing it into the cockpit. Then he straightened and kneaded tight muscles at the back of his neck, thinking furiously. Finally he turned to nail her with a glare.

"This doesn't have anything to do with me," he told her as flatly and uncompromisingly as possible.

"You gave me the courage."

Not what he wanted to hear. He said a rude word. "Don't be stupid."

"You told me not to regret my life."

"I didn't expect you to turn it upside down!"

"Maybe I'm turning it right side up," she suggested.

He raked fingers through his hair. He supposed he had said some damn stupid thing like that. Giving her the benefit of his own regrettable experience, no doubt. And she, foolishly, interpreted it as him having some common sense.

"So everyone left and you just walked up to him and said, 'Oh, by the way, Gerry, I can't marry you'?"

She looked taken aback at his tone, not understanding what the problem was. Of course she didn't understand—because the problem was his, not hers.

"I wasn't quite that blunt," she said at last. "It just… happened." She gave him a sort of sad reflective smile. "He'd said he wanted to discuss things between us—about the wedding. He wanted to set a date—a specific time. And—" she shook her head helplessly "—I couldn't do it."

He stared at her for a long moment. Then he said again, "Not because of me."

A tiny line appeared between her brows for a moment. And then she seemed to realize what he was getting at. "You mean, did I suddenly realize I'd rather have you?" She laughed. "I'm not that presumptuous."

"Good," he said gruffly, embarrassed at having made the leap at the same time he was relieved it had been in error.

"Well, good for you," he said finally, at length. What was he supposed to say? He gave her a quick approving nod, then climbed down into the cockpit, unlocked the door to the companionway and kicked his duffel down into the cabin.

"It is good," she said, her voice brighter now. "It was the right thing to do." Behind him Demetrios heard her take an expansive breath. "In fact, it feels wonderful."

He grunted. He supposed it must. Like dodging a bullet. The way he'd feel if he'd never married Lissa. He glanced up at her. "Congratulations."

She grinned. "Thank you."

He cocked his head, considering how simple it had been. Maybe too simple? "And Gerard was okay with your breaking it off?"

"Well, not exactly," she admitted. She shoved a tendril of hair that had escaped her ponytail away from her ear. "He said all brides have jitters. That I should think things over. Take some time. Get to know my own mind." She snorted—a ladylike snort. "I do know my own mind."

Did she? Demetrios doubted it. She'd agreed to marry Gerard, hadn't she? She must have thought it was a good idea at one point. And Gerard obviously expected her to come to her senses.

"And your father?" Demetrios demanded. "What did he say?" When she didn't answer at once, he narrowed his gaze. "You did tell him?"

Anny tossed her ponytail. "I sent him an e-mail."

Demetrios gaped. "You sent your father—*the king*—an e-mail?"

She shrugged, then squared her shoulders and lifted her chin defiantly. "He might be everyone else's king, but he's my father. And I didn't want to talk to him."

"I'll bet you didn't."

"He'll understand. He loves me."

No doubt he did. But he was also king of a country. A man who was used to ruling, commanding, telling everyone—especially his daughter—what to do. And he had told her to marry Gerard.

"He'll get used to it." But Demetrios thought Anny's words were more to convince herself, not him. "It will just take a little time. He might be…upset…at first, but—" another shrug "—that's why I'm leaving."

He looked up at her. "What do you mean, leaving?"

Anny turned and hopped back down onto the deck, and for

the first time Demetrios noticed the backpack and the suitcase sitting on the far side of the dock.

As he watched, she shouldered the pack, then picked up the suitcase. "I'm going away for a while."

He came to rest his elbows on the back of the cockpit and stare at her. "You're leaving Cannes?"

She nodded grimly. "Papa will be on my doorstep as soon as he gets the e-mail, finds his pilot, and fuels the jet. I don't intend to be here when he comes." She shrugged. "He will need time to come to terms. So I'm off. I just—" she smiled at him "—didn't want to leave without telling you, saying thank you."

Frankly, he thought she was carrying the etiquette a bit too far. And *You're welcome* didn't seem much of an answer. Whatever advice he'd given her had been based on his messed-up marriage and might have nothing to do with hers. What the hell had he thought he was doing?

"Maybe you should give it some time," he said now. "Don't be too hasty. Think for a while, like Gerard said. Then decide."

She stared at him as if he'd lost his mind. "I'm not being hasty. And I *have* thought! We've been engaged three years. First I wanted to finish grad school. Then I wanted to finish my dissertation." She paused, then met his gaze squarely. "I did decide, Demetrios. I think I decided—in my gut—a long time ago, which is why I kept putting it off. You're just the one who gave me the courage to say it."

They stared at each other until finally, abruptly, Anny stepped back and gave him a small salute. She smiled. "'Bye, Demetrios. Thanks for the courage." The smile broadened. "And the memories."

Then she squared her slender shoulders, shifted the backpack slightly, picked up the suitcase, and marched back up the dock toward La Croisette.

Demetrios stared after her, unmoving, while his brain whirled with fifty thousand sane reasons to turn around and start getting the boat ready to sail.

But not one of them was proof against the fear of what could happen to her if he did.

Damn it!

"Anny!" He vaulted out of the cockpit, then scrambled off the boat onto the dock. "Where are you going?"

A small figure halfway down the dock turned back. She shrugged. "I don't know yet."

She didn't sound as if it mattered.

Demetrios knew it did. His stomach clenched. Scowling now, annoyed that she could be so blasé about something that important, he stalked down the dock after her. "What do you mean, you don't know?"

He knew the hard edge to his voice made her eyes widen, but she didn't shrink away from him.

She simply set the suitcase down and faced him. "Exactly what I said. I haven't a clue. I just need to go somewhere Papa won't expect me to be. He'll look in all the places, the likely places," she allowed. "So I'll just go someplace else. It's not like I made plans, you know."

He knew. And he didn't like it one bit. She was a young woman alone. Kind, trusting. Not to mention rich—and a princess, besides. She'd be prey for more unsavory characters than he wanted to think about.

"I thought I might hitchhike," she said blithely in the face of his ominous silence.

"*Hitchhike!*" He spat the word, furious.

She burst out laughing. "I'm not going to hitchhike, Demetrios," she assured him. "I was joking. You looked so intense. I'll be fine. Don't get so worked up."

"I'm not worked up!" He was very calmly going to strangle her.

She was still smiling. "Right. Okay. You're not worked up." She gave him a sideways assessing look. Then she tried more reassurance. "You don't need to worry. You *are* worrying," she pointed out in case he hadn't noticed.

"Because you're acting like an idiot! You don't just pack up and head out at the drop of a hat. You need plans. A place to go. Bodyguards!"

She blinked. "Bodyguards?"

"You're a princess!"

"I haven't had a bodyguard since I left university. I'm perfectly capable of taking care of myself." She smiled again. It was a regal smile. It made Demetrios's teeth ache they were grinding together so hard.

"But thank you for your concern," she added, in that proper bloody well-brought-up royal tone of voice she could put on when she wanted to. Then, as if he were some mere peasant she'd just dismissed, she picked up the suitcase and started away again.

Demetrios muttered something unprintable under his breath, then stalked after her and grabbed her by the arm, hauling her to a stop. "Then you're coming with me."

Her head whipped around. She stared at him, eyes wide, mouth agape. "With you? To Greece?"

"Why not?" he demanded. "You don't have a plan of your own. You can't just wander around Europe. It's not safe."

"I'm not a fool, Demetrios. I went to Oxford by myself. I went to Berkeley!"

"With watchdogs," he reminded her.

"I was young then. Almost a child. I'm not a child now."

"No. You're a raving beauty and any man with hormones can see that!"

"I meant I'm not going to be anyone's prey."

"Right. You're big and strong and tough. That's why I practically kidnapped you right in the middle of a hotel lobby!"

"You did not!"

"I walked off with you!"

"Because I *let* you. I knew who you were. I could have screamed," she told him haughtily.

He snorted. "Everyone would have thought you were an over-excited fan."

"I can take care of myself. I don't get into cars with strangers. I don't make foolish decisions."

"Really?" He gave her a sardonic look. "You were going to marry Gerard. You propositioned me. You went to bed with me."

She glared at him. "Up until now, I didn't consider that a foolish decision."

"Think again." He dragged a hand through his hair. "Look. You're a damned appealing woman, princess. You swept me off my feet, didn't you?" he said.

She made a face at him. "I promise you, you were the one and only. Besides, I've got my memories now."

He didn't let himself think about that. "What if someone else wants a few of his own? If anything happens to you out in the big bad world, it will be my fault!"

"Don't be ridiculous. You have an outrageous sense of your own importance. What I do is my responsibility, not yours."

"But you owe it to me," he reminded her. "You said you did. That's what you came down here for—*to thank me*!"

Anny folded her arms across her breasts and glowered at him. "Obviously a mistake. So much for etiquette."

"Next time don't be so damn polite." He picked up her suitcase, then hung on determinedly as she tried to grab it out of his hand. "This is going to look great on all the paparazzi shots," he reminded her silkily.

Abruptly, she let go and glanced around, looking hunted, then annoyed. "There are no photographers!"

He shrugged, unrepentant. "There could be. You want them following you all over Europe? Bet Papa can ask them where you're hiding." He gave her a mocking look over his shoulder and kept walking.

For a long moment he was afraid she'd just let him go off with her suitcase while she went in the other direction. But finally he heard her footsteps coming after him.

"This is insane," she told him. "You don't want me with you."

"More than I want you dead in the gutter." He heard the explosion of breath that meant she was gearing up for another round, so he turned and forestalled her. "Look, blame it on my mother. It wouldn't matter if it was really my fault or not, I'd think it was. *She'd* think it was."

"You'd tell her?"

"I wouldn't have to. She'd know."

Malena Savas had eyes in the back of her head and she knew what all of her children were thinking before they ever thought it. Demetrios knew his mother had a far greater understanding of what he'd been through these past three years than he'd ever told her. Or ever would tell her. She understood at least a part of what he'd gone through—and she didn't blame him, which he considered a miracle.

But if he left Anny alone now, she'd have his head.

"She doesn't know about me," Anny protested.

"Not yet."

Anny muttered under her breath. He just kept walking. Every step took them closer to the boat.

"I suppose it will be safer for you if I come along," she said at last.

"Safer?"

"The boat will be easier to sail if there are two of us. Although I'm sure you could do it on your own."

"I could. But, you're right," he added. If that convinced her, who was he to argue?

"Still, you said you wanted solitude," she reminded him.

"Maybe you won't talk all the time," he retorted in exasperation. She smirked. "And maybe I will."

"Then I'll put you off on Elba."

"Like Napoleon?" Her lips twitched.

"Exactly." Their gazes met. Locked. Dueled.

"Napoleon escaped," Anny said loftily.

"You won't."

"How do you know?"

"When I leave you, I'll tell your father where you are."

They were joking. But they weren't joking at the same time. He meant it—and he could tell from the look on her face that Anny knew it. Stalemate.

At long last she let out a sigh. "You're serious, aren't you? You're going to stand here and argue with me for as long as it takes."

"Not that long. I might just throw you over my shoulder and dump you in the boat."

"You wouldn't."

"Want to try me?" He gave her his best Luke St. Angier hard-ass hero look.

She narrowed her gaze at him, then she said finally, "If I come, you won't think it's because I want to go to bed with you again?"

"What?" He stared at her.

"Because I don't want you thinking I'm stalking you."

"Wouldn't matter if you did," he told her flatly. "I'm immune."

"Yes, I could tell," she said drily.

He scowled. "I didn't say I didn't enjoy sex with a beautiful woman. I said, I don't want anything more than that."

That made her blink. "Ever?"

"Never." No compromise there.

Anny cocked her head and studied him carefully, as if her scrutiny might detect cracks in his armor. He could have told her there were no cracks. Not after Lissa.

He didn't. But he stood firm and unyielding under her gaze.

"You shouldn't say 'never' like that," she told him, her tone gentle, as if she intended to comfort him. "Never is a long time and you might meet someone you love as much. Differently," she added quickly. "But as much."

Demetrios stared, jolted. But he didn't correct her misunderstanding. She only knew what the press had printed, after all. She'd got the story of their marriage that Lissa had wanted read. And after Lissa's death, he'd had nothing to gain from airing their private problems.

Saying something wouldn't change things now, either. So he just waited, let her think what she liked.

"What *about* sex?" she said abruptly

His mouth fell open. He couldn't help it. "What?"

"I'm not asking you for sex," she assured him quickly. "I just want to know what's expected."

So do I, Demetrios felt like saying because God's own truth was, if he lived to be a hundred, he doubted he would be able to predict the next words out of Princess Adriana's mouth.

"It's up to you, princess," he told her gruffly. "I can't say I didn't enjoy it. I can't say I'm not willing. But I'm not falling in love with you. So don't get your hopes up."

Color flared in her cheeks. "As if!"

He grinned, then shrugged. "Just saying. You brought it up. Fine. If this is going to work, we need some plain speaking. I'm telling you right now I'm not getting involved. I'm bringing you along to keep you safe. Period."

"Whether I like it or not," she said in a mocking tone of her own.

"Whether you like it or not," he agreed. "As for sex—" he shrugged "—I have no expectations. Whatever happens on board, princess, is entirely up to you."

She blinked. Then she seemed to consider that. Her brow actually furrowed and she thought about it for long enough that Demetrios had time to wonder what the hell she could possibly be thinking.

But then she smiled, nodded and stuck out her hand. "Deal."

Out of the frying pan.

Into the fire.

Her life was turning into one big cliché.

Anny knew she should have said no. She should have turned and walked away and kept right on walking.

More to the point, she should never have come down to the harbor to find Demetrios in the first place.

She had because…because, she forced herself to admit, he was the only one she knew who would understand. He was, as she'd told him, the one who had given her the courage to do it.

He and Franck.

But she could hardly talk to Franck about this. She was supposed to be his support, not the other way around. She hadn't been expecting support, per se, from Demetrios, either. Well, nothing beyond a "good for you," which in fact he'd given her.

That was all she was hoping for. *All*! She had definitely not expected Demetrios to insist that she come with him.

She ventured a glance at him now as he prepared to leave the harbor. He was paying her no attention at all. He was stowing gear and checking charts and going over things that Anny knew were important and knew equally well she would be in the way of if she tried to help.

So she kept out of the way and waited until he gave her directions. She was by no means a solo sailor. But she'd been on boats since she was a child. And while Mont Chamion's royal yacht had a very competent crew, she had taken orders from her father when he and she and her mother had gone sailing. She was sure she could help Demetrios here.

That wasn't going to be the problem.

She wasn't a fool, Anny had been at pains to assure him. But what else could you call a woman who went from a three-year engagement to a man she didn't love to a two-week solo boat trip with a man who would never love her?

Not, Anny assured herself, that she was in love with him.

But she wasn't indifferent to him.

She…liked him. Had once had a crush on him. He had, as she'd told him in somewhat vague terms, been the dream of her youth.

And even now she respected him for his career. She admired him for coming back from the devastating personal tragedy that had been his wife's death. She certainly esteemed him for his kindness to Franck over the past couple of weeks, and—let's be honest—for his generosity to her. In and out of bed.

But she didn't love him. Not yet.

Not ever, Anny told herself sharply.

She was, despite what her dutiful engagement to Gerard might say about her, basically a sensible woman. She didn't dare fate or walk in front of buses.

Now she considered herself warned. It was more than a little humbling to hear him spell out his indifference in such blunt terms. As if there were no way on earth he might ever fall in love with the likes of her.

Fine. So be it.

Right now she was looking for a respite—some peace and quiet and a chance to learn the desires of her own heart.

So she would take what he offered: two weeks of solitude

during which her father would never be able to find her. Two weeks to formulate plans that would allow her to make her own way in her adult life.

Yes, marriage, she was sure, would be a part of it. But not marriage to Gerard. Despite his suggestion that she take some time and reconsider, Anny knew she'd made the right decision. She only regretted that it had taken her so long to come to her senses and realize she needed more than duty and responsibility to get her to the altar.

She'd suspected it, of course. But it had taken her night with Demetrios to show her that passion, too, had to play a part.

The passion, the desire, hadn't dissipated since that night.

How she was going to handle that for the next two weeks, she wasn't sure. Had he meant it when he said it was up to her?

Demetrios started the engine. The boat's motor made the deck vibrate beneath Anny's feet.

"Hey, princess, cast off." Demetrios was at the wheel, but he jerked his head toward the line still wrapped around the cleat at the stern.

Anny clambered off, unwound the line, and jumped back aboard.

He throttled the engine ahead. The boat began to move slowly out of the slip. Anny felt the cool morning breeze in her face, smelled the sea, felt a heady excitement that was so much better than the dread with which she'd awakened every morning for too long.

She knew how Franck had felt when he'd gone sailing—alive.

But she knew, too, that it was a risk.

Spending two weeks alone on a sailboat with Demetrios Savas could be the closest thing to heaven, or—if she fell in love with him—to hell that Anny could imagine.

CHAPTER SIX

MALENA SAVAS, Demetrios's mother, was fond of crisp character assessments of her children. Theo, the eldest, was "the loner," George, the physicist, was "the smart one." Yiannis was "our little naturalist" because he was forever bringing home snakes and owls with broken wings. Tallie was, of course, "baby girl."

And Demetrios, her gregarious, charming middle child?

"Impulsive," his mother would say fondly. "Kindhearted, honorable. But, dear me, yes, Demetrios tends to leap before he looks."

Apparently that hadn't changed, the middle child in question thought irritably now as he edged the boat out of the slip and headed her toward the open sea. You'd have thought that by the age of thirty-two he'd have got over it. His marriage to Lissa should have cured him of impetuosity once and for all.

But no. He'd actually gone after Anny—*Princess* Adriana—and insisted she spend the next two weeks on a damn sailboat alone with him!

What the hell had he been thinking?

Exactly what he'd told her—that sweet and kind and innocent, she was far too trusting to be let out on her own. And that it was his fault.

Not the sweet and kind and trusting bit—that was Anny. But the "out on her own bit" he felt responsible for. Hell, she'd *thanked* him for making it possible!

So he'd opened his mouth—and now here she was, standing

in the cockpit waiting for him to tell her what to do. She was smiling, looking absolutely glorious in the early morning light, the light breeze tangling her hair. He remembered its softness when his own fingers had tangled in it.

They'd happily tangle in it again. And more. But fool that he was, while he'd insisted she be on his boat for two weeks, he'd left the sleeping arrangements up to her!

Refusing to think about it, Demetrios concentrated on getting the boat out into open water. He tried not to look at her at all. But if he so much as turned his head, there she was.

"Maybe you should take your stuff below," he said, "in case anyone does recognize you while we're still in the harbor." Barely a creature was stirring on the docks or on any of the boats. But all it took was one nosy person… "I'll call you when I need your help with the sail."

She smiled. "Thanks." And picking up her suitcase, she started to carry it down the companionway steps. They were too steep. He started to offer to help, but Anny simply dropped it down the steps with a thud. Then she and her backpack disappeared after it.

Well, she was resourceful. He would give her that. And he breathed easier when she was below. It was almost possible— for a few seconds at a time—to pretend that he was still alone on the voyage.

But then as he moved beyond the harbor, he spotted the royal yacht of Val de Comesque on its mooring. And as he motored slowly past it, Demetrios could see the crew were already up and stirring.

Was Gerard up, too? Was he prowling the decks worrying about Anny?

Or did he simply think she'd gone home, gone to bed and would come to her senses in short order?

According to Anny, he'd said for her to think about it. Obviously he was confident she'd change her mind. She had sounded confident she would not.

But was that true or mere momentary bravado?

Demetrios wasn't surprised she'd balked. But he didn't

share her confidence when it came to being sure she wouldn't change her mind.

It was one thing to say you weren't going to marry a powerful wealthy, admittedly kind man like Prince Gerard and another thing to hold fast to the notion.

Maybe she really did just need time to think, to be sure.

Sure, yes? Or sure, no?

Not his problem, Demetrios told himself firmly. He believed she was right to take the time and consider her options. God knew he should have taken a couple of weeks to think about what he was doing when he'd married Lissa!

He might have come to his senses. Something else he wasn't going to think about. Too late now.

He drew a deep breath of fresh sea air and shut Lissa out of his mind. She was the past. He had a future ahead of him.

He had a new screenplay to work on. And two weeks of sea time to ponder it.

And, heaven help him, Anny.

"Anny!" He shouted her name now that they were well past the royal yacht.

Instantly she appeared in the companionway, looking at him expectantly.

"Still want to help?"

"Of course." She scrambled up into the cockpit.

He nodded at the wheel. "Steer this course while I hoist the sail."

Her eyes widened in surprise. "Steer?" She looked surprised, then delighted, stepping up to put her hands on the wheel. Her face was wreathed with a smile.

"You do know what you're doing?" he said a little warily.

"I think so," she said. "But usually no one wants me to do it. 'Can't let the princess get her hands dirty.' That sort of thing."

"For the next couple of weeks, you'll have dirty hands," he told her.

"Fine with me. I'm happy to help. Delighted," she said with emphasis. "I was just…surprised." She shot him a grin. "But thrilled."

Her grin was heart-stopping. Eager. Apparently genuine. It spoke of the sort of enthusiasm that he'd once dreamed Lissa would show toward their sailing trip to Mexico.

"Show me," she demanded.

So he showed her the course he was sailing and how to read it on the GPS. She asked questions, didn't yawn in his face and file her fingernails, and nodded when he was finished. "I can do that," she said confidently.

He hoped so. "Just keep an eye on the GPS," he told her, "and do what you need to do with the wheel. I can straighten it out if you have a problem."

"I won't," she swore.

He went forward to hoist the sail, pausing to shoot her a few quick apprehensive glances, hoping she really did know what she was doing.

She seemed to have no qualms about the task, keeping her eye on the GPS and her hand on the wheel. She had pulled on a visor of Theo's that hid most of her face from him, but as he watched, she tipped her head back and lifted her face so that the sun touched it. His breath caught at the sight.

Demetrios was accustomed to beautiful women. He'd worked with them, he'd directed them. He'd been married to one.

Flawless skin, good bones, perfect teeth all mattered. But facial features were only a part of real beauty. The superficial part. And Anny had them.

But more than that, she had a look of pure honest joy that lit her face from within. It was an uncommon beauty. *She* was an uncommon beauty.

She was also a princess who had just made a serious, life-changing decision if she decided it was the right one to make. She didn't know her own mind.

Demetrios knew his. However beautiful, sexy and appealing she was, he wasn't getting involved with her.

But he was already beginning to realize that unless Anny decided to share his bed it was going to be a very long two weeks.

* * *

Anny was exultant, loving every minute, beaming as the sun touched her face and the breeze whipped through her hair.

She felt free—blessedly unburdened by duty and responsibility for the moment at least. She had also forgotten how much she loved to get out on the water and really sail.

Her most recent experiences on boats had all been parties like the one on Gerard's yacht last night. They were so elegant and controlled that they might as well have been in hotel dining rooms. If she hadn't had to take the launch to get to the yacht and back, she would have forgotten she was even on a boat.

It certainly hadn't been going anywhere.

Now she was moving. The boat, once Demetrios had the mainsail and jib raised, was cutting through the water at a rate of knots, and Anny gripped the wheel, exhilarated. It was glorious.

When he dropped into the cockpit beside her she relinquished the wheel, but couldn't act as if it was no big deal.

"I feel alive!" she said over the wind in her ears. "Reborn!" And she arched her back, opened her arms wide and spun around and around, drinking in the experience. "Thank you! Thank you, thank you, thank you!"

He gave her a sceptical, wary look—one that reminded her of the way he'd looked at her the night she'd asked him to make love to her, that said he was seriously concerned that she'd lost her mind.

"Don't worry about me!" she said, beaming. "Truly!"

Demetrios still looked sceptical, but he didn't reply, just moved his gaze from the GPS to the horizon, then made adjustments as required.

Anny stood watching, drinking in the sight of him as eagerly as she did the whole experience. She'd seen him in a number of roles in films over the years. He'd done slick and sophisticated, hard-edged and dangerous, sexy and imbued with deadly charm. She'd seen him in a lot of places—big cities, high deserts, dense jungles, and bedrooms galore—but she'd never seen him at sea before.

It was a perfect fit. He looked competent in whatever role he played. But he wasn't playing a role now, and he seemed perfectly suited to the task.

"I didn't realize you were such a sailor," she said.

He shrugged, keeping his eyes on the horizon "Grew up sailing. We always have. It's bred in the bone, I guess." There was a slight defensive edge to his tone that surprised her.

She smiled. "I can see that," she said. "Lucky you."

Now he slanted a glance her way, his brows raised as if her comment surprised him. "It doesn't appeal to everyone. Some people find it boring."

It was her turn to be surprised at that. "I can't imagine," she said sincerely. "It seems liberating to me. Maybe it's because, being…who I am—" she could never bring herself to say "being a princess" "—when I was home as a child, I always felt hemmed in. But when my parents and I went sailing—even on one of the lakes—it was like we suddenly could be ourselves."

"Getting away from it all." He nodded.

"Yes. Exactly."

"I didn't think of it that way until I'd been 'famous'—" his mouth twisted on that word the way hers would have if she'd said "princess" "—for a while. But I know what you mean. I thought getting out and sailing was a way of getting back to who I was…." His voice rose slightly at the end of the statement as if he were going to say more. But he didn't. He just lifted his shoulders and looked away again.

"Did you have time to sail much?"

He shook his head. "Not often. Once." Something closed up in his expression. His jaw tightened. Then he fixed her with his green gaze. "Did you get everything sorted out below? Unpacked? Settled in? It's not a palace."

The change of subject was abrupt, as was the sudden rough edge to his tone. Anny wondered what caused it, and knew better than to ask.

"It's better than a palace," she told him sincerely. "I love it."

He grunted, not looking completely convinced.

"I took the back cabin—the aft cabin," she corrected herself. "It's a bit bigger, though, so if you want it, I'll be happy to switch. I just thought the forward cabin seemed more like it should be the captain's. Is that okay?"

"Fine. Whichever." He gave her a look that Anny couldn't interpret at all. Then he stared back at the horizon again, seeming lost in thoughts that had nothing to do with the situation at hand. Was he regretting having insisted she come along?

"I'll just go below for a while," she said. "If you need me again, shout."

Demetrios gave her a quick vague smile, but his mind still seemed far away. So she headed back down the companionway steps.

She had put her suitcase and laptop backpack in the aft cabin, but she hadn't unpacked them yet. Now she did, taking her time, settling in, discovering all the nooks and crannies that made living on board a boat so intriguing.

It was a gorgeous boat. Nothing like as opulent and huge as either the royal yacht of her country or of Gerard's, but it had a clean, compact elegance that made it appealing—and manageable. A good boat for a couple—or a young family like that of Demetrios's brother, Theo.

She felt a pang of envy not just for Theo's boat, but for his family. Some of her fondest early childhood memories were the afternoons spent sailing on the alpine lakes of Mont Chamion with her parents.

Now she found herself hoping that someday she and her own husband and children would do the same. Her mind, perversely but not unexpectedly, immediately cast Demetrios in the husband role. And there was wishful thinking for you, she thought.

She tried to ignore it, but her imagination was vivid and determined and would not be denied. So finally, she let it play on while she put things away.

Since she'd packed hastily in the middle of the night and had planned to escape Cannes by rail, she hadn't brought any of the right clothes. She'd assumed she would be losing herself in a big city like Paris or Barcelona or Madrid. So most of the things she'd brought were casual but sophisticated and dressy—linen and silk trousers, shell tops, jackets and skirts. Not your average everyday sailing attire.

The jeans and T-shirt she was wearing had been chosen so she could leave town looking like a student and not draw attention to herself. Unfortunately they were the only halfway suitable things she'd brought along, and in the heat of the Mediterranean summer she was nearly sweltering in them. She would need to go shopping soon.

She just hoped no one would recognize her when she did.

In the meantime she would cope. But somehow, for a woman who had spent her life learning what to do in every conceivable social situation, she had no very clear idea how to go on in this one.

Madame Lavoisier, one of her Swiss finishing school instructors, tapping her toe impatiently and repeating what she always called "Madame's rules of engagement."

"You are a guest," Madame would say. "So you must be all that is charming and polite. You may be helpful, but not intrusive. You must know how to put yourself forward when it is time to entertain, but step back—fade into the woodwork, if you will—when your hosts have other obligations. And you must never presume."

Those were the basics, anyway. You applied them to whatever situation presented itself.

And Anny could see the wisdom of it. But still it felt lacking now—because she didn't want to be a guest. She wanted to belong.

And how foolish was that?

Demetrios had told her clearly and emphatically that he wasn't interested in a relationship. He could not have made it plainer.

If she let herself get involved with him now, it would not be some fairy-tale night with a silver-screen hero. Nor would it be the adolescent fantasy of an idealistic teenager. It wouldn't have anything to do with duty and responsibility.

It would be a lifetime commitment of love to a real live flesh-and-blood man—a man who didn't want anything of the sort.

"So just have a nice two-week holiday and get on with your life," she told herself firmly.

She vowed she would. All she had to do was convince her heart.

* * *

About noon Anny brought him a sandwich and a beer.

"I figured you'd be getting hungry." She set the plate on the bench seat near where Demetrios stood, then went back down to return moments later with a sandwich of her own.

"I've been through the provisions," she told him. "Made a list of possible menus, and another of some things we should probably get when we go ashore."

He stared at her.

She finished chewing a bite of sandwich, then noticed the way he was looking at her, and said, "What? Did I overstep my bounds?"

He shook his head. "I'm just…surprised."

Anny didn't see why. "Maybe it was presumptuous," she went on after she'd swallowed, "but I'm a better cook than a sailor. And if I'm going to be here two weeks, I need to do my share. So I thought I'd do the meals."

"You cook?" That seemed to surprise him, too.

She flashed him a grin. "*Cordon Bleu*," she told him, causing his brows to hike clear into the fringe of hair that had fallen across his forehead. "All part of my royal education. But don't expect that standard under these circumstances," she warned him.

He shook his head. "No fear. I'm happy with sandwiches. I wasn't planning on cooking."

"I noticed," she said drily. Besides bread, cheese and fruit, there was little in the pantry besides granola bars and protein bars and beer.

"I wasn't expecting company." His tone was gruff. The wind was ruffling his hair, making him look dangerous and piratical and very very appealing.

"I realize that. And I'm grateful. I—" she hesitated "—appreciate your offer to bring me along. Your insistence, actually," she corrected. "It is a better alternative than wandering around Europe trying to stay a step ahead of Papa."

He nodded, then looked at her expectantly because the note on which she ended made it clear she had something else to say.

Which she did. She just couldn't seem to find the right way

to say it. Finally she simply blurted it out. "But even so, I don't think we should make love together again."

Yet another look of surprise crossed his face, this one more obvious than the earlier two. His green eyes met hers. "You don't?"

Anny gave a quick shake of her head. "No."

Demetrios tilted his head to regard her curiously. "You didn't like it?"

Anny felt her cheeks begin to burn. "You know that's not true," she protested. "You know I liked it. Very much."

He scratched his head. "And yet you don't want to do it again."

"I didn't say I didn't want to do it again. I said I didn't think we should."

He stared at her. "Your logic eludes me."

"It would mean something if we did," she explained.

He blinked. "I thought it did mean something last time. All that stuff about your idealistic youthful self…"

"Yes, of course it meant something," she agreed. "But it would be different if we did it again. That time it was…like…making love with a fantasy." Now her cheeks really did burn. She felt like an idiot, didn't want to meet his eyes. But she could feel his on her, so finally she lifted her gaze. "When we did it then, I was with the you I—I had dreamed about. The 'fantasy' you. The one I imagined. If we did it again, it wouldn't be the same. *You* wouldn't be the same. You'd be—*you*!"

"Me? As opposed to…me?" He looked totally confused now.

Anny didn't blame him. She didn't want to spell it out, but obviously she was going to have to. "You'd be a real live flesh-and-blood man."

"I was before," he told her. "Last time."

"Not the same way. Not to me," she added after a moment.

He still looked baffled. "And you don't want a 'real live flesh-and-blood man'?"

What she wanted was to jump overboard and never come up. "It's dangerous," she said.

"No, it's not. Don't worry. I won't get you pregnant. I promise. I can take care of that."

"Not that kind of dangerous. Emotionally dangerous."

He looked blank. Of course he did. He was a man.

"I could fall in love with you," she said bluntly.

"Oh." He looked appalled. "No. You don't want to do that." He was shaking his head rapidly.

No, she didn't. Not if he wasn't going to fall in love with her in return, at least. And he'd made it clear that he had no intention of doing so. She supposed there was always the chance that she could change his mind, but from the look on his face, it didn't seem likely.

"Like I said, dangerous," Anny repeated. "For me." She shrugged when he just continued to stare at her. "You said it was up to me," she reminded him.

His mouth twisted. "So I did." He rubbed a hand through his hair. "That'll teach me," he muttered.

"I'm sorry."

He made a sound that was a half laugh and half something Anny couldn't have put a name to. "Me, too, princess," he told her. Then he gave her a wry smile. "Let me know if you change your mind."

"Sure," Anny said.

But it wasn't going to happen—she hoped.

She was the most baffling woman he'd ever met.

When she didn't know him, she wanted to make love with him. When she knew him, she didn't want to—but only because she might fall in love with him.

Where the hell was the logic in that?

Well, perversely, Demetrios supposed, squinting at the Italian shoreline as if it might provide some answers, there was some. But it wasn't doing his peace of mind much good.

It made all those glimpses of Anny he kept catching out of the corner of his eye all too distracting, though he supposed she intended nothing of the sort at all.

She wasn't coy and flirtatious the way Lissa had been, eager and enthusiastic one minute, pouting and moody the next. With Lissa he'd never known where he stood or what she wanted.

With Anny, she flat-out told him.

When she wanted to make love, she'd said so. Now she didn't, and she'd said that. No, he'd never met a woman even close to her.

After their discussion, she had finished her lunch, then taken both their plates below. He'd expected she would stay there to avoid him and his "dangerous" appeal. But she came back to put her feet up on one of the cockpit benches and leaned back to lift her face. She still wore Theo's visor, but for the moment her face was lit by the sun and the wind tangled her hair.

"Isn't this glorious?" she said, turning a smile in his direction. And there really was nothing flirtatious about the smile at all. Just pure enjoyment of the moment.

"Yeah," Demetrios agreed, because it was.

But also because it was pretty damned glorious to stand there and simply watch her take pleasure in the moment. For the longest time she didn't move a muscle, didn't say a word, just sat there silently, absorbing, savoring the experience.

She didn't glance at him to see if he was noticing. Lissa had always been aware of her audience.

He remembered when she'd badgered him to take her sailing. He had been in Paris at the time and she back in L.A., having just finished a film. And every time they talked on the phone she'd chattered about how wonderful it had been going sailing with a couple of big A-list stars.

"We could go sailing," she'd said to him.

It was the first time she'd shown the least interest in any such thing. When he'd taken her to his parents' place on Long Island right after they were married, she hadn't set foot on the family boat. She'd had little to do with anyone, and she'd been eager to leave almost as soon as they'd arrived.

He'd thought at the time it was because she'd wanted to spend some more time with him alone. Only later he began to realize a family vacation on Long Island wasn't fast-lane enough for her.

But when she'd made the remark about sailing, he'd taken her suggestion at face value and offered to charter a sailboat so they could go to Cabo San Lucas as soon as he got back home.

Lissa had been delighted.

"Ooh, fun," she'd squealed on the phone when he'd tossed out the idea to her.

They hadn't seen each other for more than two days at a time in the past two months. It seemed like a great way to spend some time alone with her. And he'd been delighted she was as eager for some uninterrupted time together.

"It will be wonderful!" Lissa had crowed. And he knew that tone of voice—it was the one that went with the impossibly sparkly blue eyes. She'd let out a sigh of ecstasy. "The wind. The water. The two of us. Oh, yes. Let's. I always feel as if I'm in communion with nature."

So two days after he got home, he'd chartered a boat, and they'd set sail to Cabo from Marina del Rey.

For the first five minutes Lissa had looked exactly as content as Anny did now. But an hour later the contentment had vanished.

The wind was too cold. The boat tilted too much. The ocean spray wasn't good for her complexion. She was afraid of sunburn.

Demetrios had tried to be sympathetic. Then he'd tried to joke her out of it. But Lissa didn't take teasing at all. She pouted. She wept. She slammed around and threw things when she was upset. They weren't two hours out of Marina del Rey and she had become seriously upset.

Demetrios did his best to placate her. "I've missed you, Lis. I've been waiting for this."

She looked at him, appalled and flung her arms in despair. "This? This? There's nothing here!"

"We're here. The two of us. Alone," he reminded her. "No press. No fans. No one at all. Just us. Relax and enjoy it."

But Lissa hadn't relaxed and she hadn't enjoyed it. She'd gone below, she'd come up to the cockpit. She'd flipped through a magazine, tried to read a possible script. There was no one to talk to. She was bored.

He'd offered to let her take the wheel. She'd declined. "I wouldn't know what to do."

"I'll teach you," he'd offered.

She hadn't wanted that, either.

As the hours passed, she'd become more agitated. She hadn't been able to sit still.

"When do we get there?" she'd begun asking when they'd barely left Catalina behind. She had looked around hopefully, as if their destination might materialize on the horizon. "It's only a couple of hours to Cabo."

Demetrios had stared at her. "Flying," he'd agreed. "Sailing it'll probably take us about a week."

"A week?" Lissa's voice was so loud and so shrill he thought they probably could have heard it in Des Moines.

"Well, depending on the winds, of course, but—"

But she hadn't let him get any more out than that. She'd lit into him with a fury he'd only seen before on the set when she'd played a drug addict deprived of her source. She'd got an Emmy nomination for the performance.

It turned out she hadn't been acting. It turned out Lissa had more than a small drug habit. She'd been intending to score some in Mexico, though Demetrios hadn't known it at the time. There was a whole lot about Lissa he hadn't known then—things that even now he wished he'd never known.

It would have made it easier to forgive her. To forgive himself.

That disastrous trip had occurred just six months into their marriage. Later he'd thought it was the beginning of the slide downhill. Even that wasn't true. The slide had begun before she'd even walked up the aisle to become his wife.

He'd been fooled. Conned. Duped into believing he'd found the woman of his dreams.

Because he'd wanted it so much that he'd convinced himself? Or because Lissa had played the role so well?

How much had been intentional misdirection and how much had simply been bad judgment? Demetrios had no idea still.

All he could remember is that she'd looked so perfect on their wedding day. So content. So happy,

Anny looked that way now—happy, her eyes closed, her face in repose.

But hers was not like Lissa's version of "happy."

Lissa's "happiness" had always had an effervescence to it. She had bubbled, emoted, reacted. She had *acted* happy.

Sitting here now basking in the sunshine, eyes shut, wind in her hair, Anny wasn't acting. She simply was.

There was no bubbliness, no bounce. No reaction. Her emotion was quiet, accepting, serene—and, heaven help him, enticing in its very stillness.

Dangerously enticing.

And Demetrios understood quite clearly now what Anny meant about making love with him being "dangerous" because it would involve her heart.

Indulging these thoughts about Anny—seeing in her the antithesis of Lissa—was dangerous in the extreme. It could undermine his resolve. It could make him vulnerable.

She didn't have to entice him intentionally. It was worse, in fact, that she wasn't. It made him want things he had promised himself he would never want again.

"You're going to get a sunburn if you keep doing that," he said gruffly.

Anny's eyes flicked open in surprise. She dipped her head so that Theo's sun visor shaded her face again and she sat up straight, then smiled up at him. "You're right," she said, flexing her shoulders and stretching like a cat in the sun. "But it feels wonderful."

To his ears, her voice almost sounded like a purr. He didn't answer. He didn't know what to say in the face of such innocent happiness.

He found himself wishing she were more like Lissa so she would be easier to resist.

At the same time he couldn't help being glad she was not.

CHAPTER SEVEN

CINDERELLA ONLY GOT a single evening to indulge her fantasy.

Anny had had her evening with Demetrios. But now, amazingly, it seemed as if she was going to get two whole weeks.

Two weeks to be simply herself—not a princess, not Gerard's fiancée. Just plain Anny. With no demands, no expectations at all.

Not even sex.

Not that she wouldn't have liked to enjoy sex with Demetrios. The one night she'd spent with him had been astonishing, revelatory, incomparable.

It had made her want more.

Too much more.

So much more that she had not dared to allow herself to think about it. Limiting it to one night and walking away had been possible. But indulging herself in the joy of spending two weeks of nights in his bed, in his arms, would not work.

She would want more than those two weeks.

She would want a lifetime of them. And not just of making love with Demetrios, but of being loved by him.

She wasn't there yet. But she would be if she allowed herself to give into the temptation. And so she'd said, "No sex."

She hadn't explained it well. She wasn't sure that she could ever explain it so that it made sense to him. He was a man. Men didn't think about sex the same way. And he clearly had no problem enjoying sex with her and then walking away without a backward glance.

He'd basically promised to do just that.

Well, more power to him, Anny thought wryly. She knew her own limitations. And she knew they precluded that. So she said she was sorry and she stuck to her guns.

Having made her statement, though, she went below to work on her dissertation for a while. It seemed a good idea to give Demetrios some space to get used to a platonic two weeks.

Apparently it didn't bother him at all because when she came back out on deck late that afternoon, he was perfectly cheerful and equable—as if it didn't matter to him a bit.

Which she supposed it didn't. Which served her right, Anny supposed, telling herself it was all for the best.

"When do you want to eat dinner?" she asked him.

"Up to you."

"Are you planning to sail through the evening or moor somewhere?"

He gestured toward the shoreline. "There's a small village with a protected harbor up ahead. We'll moor there. Too much work to sail overnight. And what's the point?"

She completely agreed. "Then I'll plan on dinner for after we're tied up."'

"Sounds good." He slanted her a grin that made her heart beat a bit faster.

"Will you be going ashore?" she asked him.

He shook his head. "Not unless you want something."

She could use some clothes that were more appropriate for sailing. But she didn't want to go ashore to get them. Not in a small village not so very far from her own country. Too many people might recognize her around here. And they would certainly recognize Demetrios. He was famous the world over.

"No," she decided. "Call me if you need help," she said, knowing full well he wouldn't. Then she went back below and put together a salad and some bruschetta to go with the bread, then sliced some meat and cheese.

She was just setting the table when she heard him call her name.

Startled, Anny climbed quickly up the steps and saw that they were coming into the harbor.

"Come take the wheel while I bring down the sail," Demetrios commanded.

She blinked in surprise. But apparently he'd taken her offer at face value and was now looking at her expectantly. So she did what she was told.

"Theo would be a purist and skip the engine," Demetrios muttered as he started it up. Then he shrugged. "But I'm not as good at it as he is."

He seemed fine at it to Anny. His quick efficient competence as he hove to, then brought the mainsail down over the boom, seemed nothing short of miraculous to Anny. She hung on to the helm and tried to keep the boat where he wanted it as he finished furling the jib.

And she was just congratulating herself on doing her bit and handing the wheel back over to him, when he said, "Get up on the bow. I need you to signal me which side the buoy is on and then tie on to the mooring ball."

"Me?"

Something unreadable flickered in his gaze. Anny didn't even try to figure it out. She just said, "Right," and scrambled up to do what he asked.

Using her hand signals to guide him, Demetrios adjusted the course, backing down the motor as they closed in on the buoy. "Okay. Grab the mooring line," he instructed.

She grabbed it, then, continuing to follow his directions, she passed the bridle line through the eye, and quickly, trying not to fumble, wrapped the other end securely to the bow cleat. Then she sat back on her heels and waited for something dire to happen.

Nothing did. Or if it did, she was too inept to tell.

But then Demetrios called, "Great. That's it."

"It is?" she asked cautiously.

A quick glance at him and she saw a grin lighting his face. It was as if she'd been awarded some distinguished medal. At his thumbs-up, Anny took a deep breath and let it out again in a whoosh. She flexed her shoulders and grinned back at him. A warm elemental sense of satisfaction filled her.

The feeling was closest, she supposed, to the satisfaction she felt when she figured out a bit more of the culture and history of the cave painters she was writing her dissertation about. It was as if a significant piece of the puzzle fell into place.

She felt like that now.

But this was more. Now she felt a physical satisfaction as well. She hadn't done much of the sailing today. But she'd done more physical work than she ordinarily did. She was tired, her muscles had been challenged by the unaccustomed exertion. Her skin was a bit sunburned even in spite of the lotion she'd slathered on exposed body parts and the visor she wore. She felt alive, aware. Wonderful.

Free.

She opened her arms and spun around, embracing the whole world in the joy of it.

"That good, is it?" Anny heard Demetrios's amused voice behind her.

She felt faintly embarrassed by her childish exuberance, but not embarrassed enough to pretend complacency. She turned and smiled at him. "It's the best day I've had in years."

His brows lifted and he looked at her a long moment, as if he were trying to determine if she was sincere. She met his gaze squarely, unapologetically.

Finally, slowly, a heart-stoppingly gorgeous smile lit his face. "Then that is good," he said. "I'm glad."

He was glad he'd brought her along.

It was better than being alone.

All the time he'd been at Cannes, he'd longed for time alone. But he knew that if he'd been here alone, he'd have been restless. He would have sailed happily enough. But he would have spent most of the time in his head thinking about work, about the new screenplay, about the distribution deal he'd just done. He would not have appreciated the moment.

Now he couldn't help it.

It was hard not to with Anny embracing it every time he looked at her.

And he did look at her. A lot.

From the first day he'd met her, she had stirred something in him that he thought Lissa had killed. Not just his desire for sex—though admittedly Lissa had done a number on him there, too.

But Anny's whole outlook on life was so different.

Of course it would be, he could hear Lissa scoff in his mind. Princess Adriana had never had the disadvantage of growing up illegitimate in tiny, dusty Reach, North Dakota. Princess Adriana had always had everything her little heart desired. Why shouldn't she embrace life? It gave her everything she wanted.

Yes, he had known Lissa well enough to know exactly what she would have said about Anny. It was what she said about everyone. No one had ever had things as tough as Lissa. No one had overcome as much, had suffered more.

Admittedly his late wife had overcome her fair share of obstacles. But some of them, Demetrios knew, were of her own making. Some of them were the product of the chip on her shoulder she could never quite shake off.

"Why should I?" she'd said to him once. "It's made me who I am."

For better or worse, yes, it had. And what he knew above all was that it had never made her happy. She'd never felt joy like Anny had expressed tonight. She'd never opened her arms and embraced life.

"You're very pensive," Anny said to him now.

They were eating dinner on deck. She'd brought their salads, meat and cheese up to the cockpit because, as she'd said, "Why be down below when it's so glorious up here?"

They'd enjoyed the sunset while they'd eaten, and his mind had drifted back to the miserable nights he'd spent sailing to Cabo with Lissa, and how different it had been from this.

"Is something wrong?" Anny asked him. "They don't look like good thoughts."

He flexed his shoulders. "Just thinking how much better this is than the last time I went sailing."

"I thought you went with your brother and Franck," she said, frowning.

"I meant the last time I went a few years ago." But he smiled as he remembered the very last time. "When we went with Franck it was good."

"He thought so," she agreed. "I wish he could do more of it. Mostly he won't leave his room." She paused thoughtfully. "It's easier not to, I think."

"Yes." It was definitely easier not to risk. Safer, as well not to want what you couldn't have.

Demetrios drained his beer and stood up. "You cooked. I'll clean up."

"You worked hard all day," Anny said, standing, too. "I'll help." And carrying her plate, she followed him down into the galley.

She was no help. Not to his peace of mind, anyway. Oh, she washed plates and put away food. But the galley was small—too small for them not to bump into each other. Too small for him to avoid the whiff of flowery shampoo, the occasional brush of her hair as she dodged past him to get to the refrigerator, and— once—the outright collision that brought his chest and her breasts firmly against each other.

He remembered her softness. Wanted to feel it again.

The more time he spent with her, the more he wanted to spend. And, let's face it, the closer he wanted to spend it. He wanted to touch her fresh, soft skin. He wanted to thread his fingers through her hair. Wanted to carry her off to his bunk and know her even more thoroughly than he'd known her the one time he'd made love with her.

But it wasn't going to happen.

She'd said so. Had explained why. He understood. He just wished his hormones did.

He stepped back out of the galley and said abruptly, "Not going to work."

Anny blinked at him. "What's not?"

"This." He jerked his head toward her in the galley. "You can clean up or I will. Not both of us."

"But—"

If she were Lissa, all this brushing and bumping would have been a deliberate tease. Not with Anny. Now he just looked at her and waited for the penny to drop.

He could tell the moment that it did. Instead of looking at him coquettishly and giving him an impish smile as Lissa would have done, Anny looked mortified.

"You think I—" Her face flamed. She shook her head. "I never—! I'm sorry. I shouldn't have— Oh God!"

"It's all right," he said. "I can control myself. But I'd rather do the cleaning up myself."

Her cheeks were still bright red. "Of course," she mumbled, and she practically bolted up the companionway steps without a backward glance.

Demetrios watched her go. It was a tempting view.

He didn't need the temptation, God knew, but there were some things a man simply couldn't resist.

As the days went on it wasn't only the physical Anny that Demetrios found hard to resist. She was as appealing as ever physically.

But it was something more that attracted him. She was cheerful, bright, thoughtful, fun. And he never knew what she was going to do next.

One afternoon she decided she'd fish for their dinner. He scoffed at the notion. "You fish?"

"What? You think princesses can't fish?"

"Not in my experience."

"Known a lot of princesses, have you?"

"One or two," he told her. That one had been five and the other ninety-five didn't seem worth mentioning.

"Well, live and learn," she told him, putting the rod together and settling down on the deck. "We used to go fishing on Lake Isar in Mont Chamion. We had our own little hideaway there, a little rustic cabin my great-grandfather built."

"No castle?" he teased.

She shook her head, smiling, but her expression softened and she got a faraway look in her eyes. "About as far from a palace as you can get and still have indoor plumbing. Grandfather had that put in," she told him. "We loved it there—Mama, Papa and I—because we could be ourselves there. Not royal, you know?"

He didn't, of course. Not about the "royal" bit. But Demetrios nodded anyway because since he'd become famous he'd learned all about the need to get away.

"It was the perfect place," Anny went on. "Quiet. Solitary. Calm. I felt real there. Myself. My family. No distractions."

"Except the fish."

She grinned. "Except the fish."

"I presume you brought bait for the fish there—which is going to be something of a problem here." He nodded at the bare hook on the end of her line.

"Sometimes we did," she agreed. "Sometimes, though," she added saucily, "we used whatever was handy. Like now." And she dug into her pocket and pulled out a tin of sardines she'd found below.

Demetrios laughed. "If you catch a fish with that, princess, I'll cook it."

She laughed, too. Then she baited her hook and cast the line over the side. It was less than half an hour later that he heard her say, "I got one!"

It was a sea bass, Demetrios told her. *Spignola.* "Good eating," he said, taking if off the hook and heading down to the galley.

"I can cook it," Anny protested.

But he insisted. Once they moored the boat for the evening, she stayed on deck and kept fishing, he baked it with a bit of olive oil, lemon, tomatoes, and basil.

"Nothing fancy. Just something I learned at my mother's knee," he said when he brought the plates up on deck. He'd torn up greens for a salad and had two beer bottles tucked under his arm.

"Did you cook a lot?"

"No. But she made sure we all knew our way around a kitchen."

Anny thought she'd like to meet Demetrios's mother. She didn't say so. But she did ask about his mother and father and what it had been like growing up in a family of seven.

"A madhouse," he said. But the expression on his face told her the memories were good ones. "We were wild. Crazy. We rode bikes off roofs. We fell out of trees. We climbed up the sides of public buildings because we could. My mother said we'd all end up dead or in jail."

"Surely not!" Anny couldn't keep the shock out of her voice even as she envisioned a horde of obstreperous little boys.

Demetrios grinned. "She's given to hyperbole, my mother."

"Ah. Well, I think it must have been nice having all those built-in playmates."

He took a swallow of the beer and smiled wryly. "Sometimes. When we weren't trying to kill each other."

"You were lucky," she decided, even after he regaled her with half a dozen more stories that ended with either him or one of his brothers, usually George, in the emergency room.

"We pounded on each other quite a bit," he said with considerable relish.

"Like I said, you're lucky."

Then, for contrast, she told him about growing up in Mont Chamion, about what it was like to be "royal." There was no pounding. No emergency room visits—except once when she had an ingrown toenail. What there were were expectations.

"Duties," she said. "Responsibilities. Selflessness. Not that there's anything wrong with that," she added quickly. "But being a doctoral candidate is a lot easier. The hopes of a country don't ride on my dissertation."

"But they do when you're a princess." It wasn't a question.

But she pulled up her knees and wrapped her arms around them and answered it anyway. "Sometimes it seems like that."

"Like marrying Gerard."

"Yes." She nodded slowly, trying to find words to explain. "It's tricky, doing the right thing—for yourself and for your country. You have to learn to walk a very careful line. I'm still learning."

Demetrios was silent then in the face of her confession, and Anny didn't know what he was thinking. When she'd first tacked his poster up on her wall all those years ago, she'd imagined she knew him perfectly. She'd dared to believe, based on his acting roles and the few interviews she'd read, that she knew and understood him. She'd dreamed of a relationship with him.

Now she realized how little she had known him, how much better she knew him now. How much more she still wanted to know. "What about you?"

He flexed his shoulders. "What about me?" He sounded as if he didn't want to talk any more about himself, but she persisted.

"You got to choose your work. Is being a director what you always wanted to do?"

"You mean besides being a fireman or a cowboy?" The answer was pat—every little boy's dream—and so was the grin on his face. It was the grin from the poster boy.

Anny widened her eyes, considering him with mock seriousness. "I think you still could be," she told him gravely, "if you really want to."

He blinked, looking briefly nonplussed, then realized she was joking and laughed.

She laughed, too, but asked again, "No, really, Demetrios. What did you want?"

She thought he wasn't going to answer her he was so quiet again, and for a very long time. But then he let out a breath and said slowly, "I don't know. I guess I just sort of thought I'd do what they did—my grandfather and my dad. You know, grow up, get married, have kids." His tone changed, grew harder, and his expression turned suddenly bleak. He shrugged. "Nothing major," he ended gruffly.

Nothing major. Except everything he wanted had been ripped away with the death of his wife. Instinctively Anny reached out a hand to touch his.

But before she could, Demetrios stood up. "Good fish. If you're finished, I'll do the washing up."

Anny scrambled to her feet as well. "It's my turn," she protested. "You cooked." *We could do it together*, she wanted to say. Wanted to believe things had changed.

Their gazes met, locked.

Then Demetrios shrugged. "Fine. You do it."

It had been easier when he felt dead—when nothing mattered, when he didn't care.

Now as he sat on the deck and stared into the darkness, all the while aware of the sounds of dish washing going on below, Demetrios wished he could tap into that zombie-like indifference again.

He didn't want to think about how much he enjoyed Anny's company. Didn't want to experience the gnawing need to learn more about her, to know about her life when she was growing up or, damn it, what her hopes and dreams were now.

And he didn't want to want more. But he did.

When the sounds in the galley ceased and the light below flicked off, he breathed a sigh of relief, grateful that she'd decided an early night was a good idea.

It wasn't that he couldn't control his hormones when he was around her. He was attracted—no denying that—but could cope. It was that somehow she made him feel human again, made him care again.

He didn't want that, either. Not at all.

"What do you know about stars?"

He jerked, turning to see Anny's silhouette as she emerged from the companionway. She handed him a glass and poured each of them a glass of wine before asking again, "What do you know about stars?"

"Most of 'em are a pain in the butt." His fingers were strangling the stem of the glass. What the hell was she doing here now?

She laughed. "Not those kinds of stars. The ones in the sky."

His mind went briefly blank. And then he shrugged. "Nothing.

I don't know anything. Just a few constellations, the North Star, a few basics I learned as a boy for navigating in the way of Greek fishermen, without instruments. Why?"

She sat down across from him. Her profile was backlit by the sprinkling of lights from the small seaside village behind her. As he watched, she took a sip of the wine, then tipped her head back and stared up into the darkness.

"When I was little," she said, "I used to wish on them."

"Lots of little kids do," he said, aware that his voice sounded rusty. He set the glass down. He did not need wine to muddy his brain tonight.

"Did you?" she asked, her voice light. "Wish on stars?"

"No. I was a tough little kid. Tough little kids don't do sissy stuff like that."

She laughed. "Right. You were very fierce."

"I was. Had to be."

"I suppose." She spoke the words quietly. She lowered her head so that she wasn't staring at the stars anymore. It felt as if she was looking at him. Assessing him.

Demetrios shrugged his shoulders against the cockpit wall and stared back, though he couldn't make out her features at all. "You have a problem with that?"

He saw her shake her head. "No. I'm just trying to know you better."

He didn't like the sound of that. "Why?"

"I thought I knew you when all I had was your poster. I was wrong. Obviously. I'm trying to remedy my ignorance." It sounded almost logical.

He grunted, which was marginally more polite than saying, "Don't bother," which would have been wiser.

"I thought if you wished on stars, maybe you'd tell me what you'd wished for. And then I could tell you what I wished for. Conversation starters, you know? It was a whole section of Swiss finishing school 101—getting to know you," she said lightly.

Demetrios chewed on the inside of his cheek. He cracked his knuckles. He rolled his shoulders. He wasn't about to talk about what he'd wished for. But he didn't mind if she did. "What did you wish for?" he asked gruffly at last.

"A brother. I hated being an only child."

"You can have any of mine," he said promptly.

He heard her laugh softly. "Thanks, but I'm not wishing for them anymore. I've got them."

"And you're okay with that?" he asked, because wanting a sibling when you were five or eight wasn't the same as getting them when you were nearly twenty. He wouldn't have been surprised if she'd resented these little interlopers who were now closer to the throne than she was.

But she just said, "It's wonderful."

"So you're fond of them?"

"I love them," she said with quiet ferocity. "I hope I have kids just like them someday." She paused and glanced up to the heavens. "I *wish* for them."

Demetrios felt an unwelcome twinge at the thought of Anny as the mother of someone's children. Whose? he wondered, then deliberately shook the thought off.

"Yeah, well, I hope you get 'em then," he said.

They sat silently after that, the boat rocking beneath them. A minute passed. Two. Then Anny said wryly, "So much for conversation starters. Your turn."

"I didn't go to Swiss finishing school," he protested.

"You only need a bit of polite curiosity. Isn't there anything you want to know?"

There were a thousand things he wanted to know—none of which he was going to ask. So he asked the one thing that had occurred to him more than once ever since they'd set sail.

"Every day it's hotter than hell. Why do you keep wearing those damn jeans?"

"Because they're all I've got."

He straightened and stared at her through the black of the night. "*What*?"

She shrugged. "Everything else is city clothes—what I thought I'd be wearing. Blazers, linen trousers, silk blouses."

"And you didn't think to mention it?"

"I didn't want to go ashore. We were near Cannes. You're too well-known everywhere. People would notice. Papa would find out."

"You don't think Papa will find out if you die of heatstroke?"

"Oh, for heaven's sake! I wouldn't have let it come to that. I didn't realize it was bothering you."

"It wasn't bothering—"

"I'll cut the trousers into shorts tomorrow."

"You can go shopping tomorrow. We'll moor some place bigger and you can go ashore without me," he said firmly.

"I don't know—"

"Don't be an idiot, princess." He hauled himself up, stalked past her and clattered down the companionway steps. Moments later he came back and threw a T-shirt and a pair of his shorts at her. "In the meantime, wear those. You can use some rope to hold them up."

Anny clutched the clothes against her, staring up at him and he was close enough now that in the sliver of rising moonlight he could see a smile on her face. "Thank you," she said. "That's very kind of you."

"Yeah, that's me. Kindness personified."

"You are. You're—"

"Tired and I want to go to sleep," he cut her off brusquely. "So unless you have any more conversation starters that can't wait, I'd appreciate it if you'd vacate my nightly resting place."

There was a split second's silence in which he expected her to take offense. But she just got up, saying, "Of course."

She picked up the bottle and the glasses, wrapping them in his shirt and shorts. Then, just as he dared to breathe a sigh of relief as she headed for the companionway, she stepped directly in front of him, rose up on her toes and brushed a kiss across his lips.

"Good night, Demetrios. Sleep well."

CHAPTER EIGHT

SLEEP WELL? Yeah, right.

Demetrios was lucky he slept at all.

He lay awake half the night, staring at the stars, his mind full of visions of Anny making her damned wishes. He had no trouble at all imagining a wistful eight-year-old leaning on the window-sill, looking up at the stars, whispering wishes as if someone would hear them—and make them come true.

How childish and unrealistic was that? He ground his teeth, flipped over onto his side and punched the pillow he'd stuck under his head. Life didn't hand you your heart's desires on a plate. No one knew that better than he did.

But you couldn't tell Anny. She'd just look at you with her sweet gentle expression and then she would smile a commiserating smile, one that said she hurt for you, that she understood.

But she didn't understand. Never would.

But that wasn't his problem, he reminded himself. Anny was who she was, and nothing would change that.

Besides, for better or worse he'd done his bit—he'd listened to her talk about marrying Gerard and he'd opened his mouth about regrets. Now he had to give her space to figure things out for herself.

Even if he went quietly crazy in the process.

His mother would tell him it was his penance for sticking his oar in where it didn't belong in the first place. Undoubtedly she was right. She would tell him to get over it. She would be right about that, too. When he was a boy, banging around the house about the injustice of it all, she would grab him by the shoulders, point him toward the door, and say, "Get out of here. Go out and burn off some of that craziness."

Abruptly he sat up, yanked his T-shirt over his head, vaulted out of the cockpit, and dived into the sea.

Sometimes mothers really did know best.

It was sunny and bright when Anny awoke. For a moment she thought she was back in her room in the palace at Mont Chamion, the only place she lived where the sun streamed in across her bed.

But then the bed rocked and she sat up, blinking. Had she slept right through Demetrios starting the engine as they left the mooring?

The sound always prompted her to yank on her jeans, button up her shirt, and run a brush through her hair so she could get up on deck quickly to help when he was ready to raise the sail.

She looked around, bewildered. Then she threw back the sheet, put on the shorts and T-shirt he'd given her last night, and hurried up the steps, only to be confronted by the dead calm of the harbor where they'd moored last night—and the sight of Demetrios Savas sprawled sound asleep on one of the cockpit benches.

She stopped dead on the steps and stared, mesmerized by the sight.

He was lying on his back, wearing only a pair of shorts. One arm was out flung, the other clutched a T-shirt against his bare chest.

Cautiously she crept closer, barely breathing as she feasted her gaze on him. She'd been to bed with him, but she'd never slept with him. Had never seen him unguarded like this.

Awake his features were always animated. Perhaps it was the actor in him, but she'd never known a man who could say so much with a simple look or draw her eyes with the lift of a brow or the twist of his gorgeous mouth.

Even in repose, he was impossible to ignore. And given a chance she'd never expected, Anny simply stood there and took him in. Her eyes traced the line of his almost perfect nose, slightly askew, she knew, because his brother George had broken it for him when he was twelve. She marveled at his dark brows and thick lashes, which should have been wasted on a man, but weren't on him. They seemed ever so slightly to soften his sharp masculine cheekbones, rough stubbled jaw, and hard mouth.

He wasn't only a pretty face, though. He also had a gorgeous body—with broad shoulders, lean hips, sinewy arms, a strong chest, and muscled hair-roughened legs. She studied him slowly, leisurely, remembering what it had been like to touch him. And what it had felt like when he'd touched her.

He had gorgeous hands with strong square-tipped fingers and callused palms. Working man's hands, Anny thought. She loved watching them raise a sail or fillet a fish or tie knots. And lover's hands. Oh, yes.

He was thirty-two years old—a man in his prime, hard and tough and uncompromising. And when he was awake that was what you saw in him. But in his sleeping face, Anny could still see hints of the younger Demetrios—the idealistic young man whose poster she'd stared at for hours on end, dreaming, wishing…

It wasn't only stars she had wished on, Anny thought wryly.

Or maybe it was that she'd wished on Hollywood stars, too. One of them, anyway. Fool that she was.

Well, she was all grown up now and trying not to wish. Trying hard. It was just very difficult.

Demetrios came awake with a start when the sun hit his eyes. He squinted, disoriented, and it only got worse when the first thing he saw was Anny watching him.

His head pounded from lack of sleep. His skin felt crusty from the dried salt on it. His shorts were still clammy and damp. And he didn't know what the hell time it was, but clearly it was later than it should have been.

"What are you staring at?"

She smiled. No surprise there. Anny smiled more than anyone he'd ever met. Honestly smiled. Not like some Hollywood actress playing a part. "You."

He groaned and scrubbed his hands over his face. "Why?"

"I like to?"

At least she made it sound like a question. "You're not sure?"

"No, I'm sure," she said matter-of-factly. "I'm just wondering why I do. You're such a grouch."

Because it was easier being a grouch. Easier to keep her at a distance. Easier to remember that he didn't want to get involved with Princess Adriana.

He shrugged. "So don't." He stood up, stretched cramped muscles, then scratched his chest and rubbed a hand through salt-stiffened hair. He should have taken a shower after his middle-of-the-night swim, but the whole point had been to wear himself out and then collapse and go to sleep. That part had worked. Finally. But now he felt like something stuck to the bottom of a fish tank. "What time is it?"

"Eight-thirty."

"Why didn't you wake me?"

She shrugged. "We're not on a schedule." She stretched her long bare legs out in front of her and he noticed that her jeans were gone and she was wearing his shorts and NYU T-shirt. She should have looked scruffy, nondescript and unappealing in them. Good luck, he thought grimly. In fact she looked bright and fresh and far too enticing for a woman who wasn't going to sleep with him.

Anny stood up, too, the morning sun graciously outlining her curves for him. "I made coffee. Do you want some?"

It was undoubtedly the best offer he was going to get. "Yeah. Let me grab a shower. Then we can get going."

The morning sun gave way to clouds by midday, something might be blowing up and bringing a storm their way before nightfall. While he kept them on course, Anny got on the radio and checked the weather reports.

"Rain and squally winds," she reported back. "This evening or tomorrow morning."

"We'll tie up midafternoon then. Give you a chance to do your shopping."

"It's not necessary now that you've lent me these." She nodded down at the shirt and shorts.

He didn't argue. But that afternoon he chose a mooring near a place big enough to have shops. It wasn't a great harbor, though. He didn't really want to ride out a storm here. As soon as they'd tied up, he readied the inflatable for her.

She didn't argue, either. She clambered into the small inflatable. She was still wearing his shirt and shorts, as well as Theo's sun visor and a pair of wraparound sunglasses. She had pulled her hair into a ponytail, which poked through the back of the visor. As a disguise, he thought it worked.

"I've got the grocery list," she said, tucking it into the pocket of the shorts. He started the small engine for her and gave her instructions about how to start it for the return trip.

She listened, nodded, then said, "I'll manage." She settled in, and Demetrios stepped back onto the sailboat, then gave the inflatable a shove to send her on her way.

"Of course you will." But as he watched the small inflatable boat chug slowly away, he cracked his knuckles, thinking that this must be what it felt like to watch your child leave home on the first day of school.

He scrubbed the deck and polished the bright work and mended a tear in the jib while she was gone. All things that needed to be done. And if they kept him up on deck so he could see the moment she got back to the inflatable, it was only to be sure she didn't have any problems getting the engine started.

She didn't. And she was beaming when he held out a hand and hauled her on board. "I brought pizza!"

"So much for *Cordon Bleu.*"

She laughed. "You'll love it." She also brought two bags with what he presumed were new clothes, and two more bags of groceries. "Come and see," she invited. Her delight in both the pizza and her shopping expedition was obvious. She was like a kid with new toys, he thought, not a princess who had everything.

Bemused, Demetrios followed, and discovered it was olives

and tomatoes and fresh bread that she was thrilled about. She seemed in no hurry to change out of his shirt and shorts.

"Here." She handed him plates. "Take them up top. We can eat on deck. I'll bring the wine."

It was hardly a feast. But Anny's simple joy made it seem like a party. She told him everything she had seen in town.

"I know it's only been a week, but I'd forgotten what it was like to be in shops and on streets. I almost got run over by a motorcyclist!"

"You need to be careful," he said, not smiling at the idea even though she was.

"I'm all right," she said cheerfully. "It was fun. And no one even looked at me twice."

He doubted that. Even deliberately cultivated anonymity would not make Anny disappear. She was too bright, too animated.

"I bought a bikini," she told him with delight, making him choke on his wine. "Let's go swimming after we finish."

"No."

She blinked. "No? But—"

"I want to sail on. We need a more sheltered harbor if it's going to storm." And he had no desire to see Anny in a bikini. His memory and his imagination were quite enough.

Anny didn't argue. She said, "Aye, aye, sir," and took the plates and dishes below to clean up.

He got them underway again and she appeared on deck to take the wheel while he raised the sail. The harbor he wanted to reach was another hour or two south, longer if they ended up sailing into the wind the whole way. He didn't know how long they had until the rains began.

The winds shifted and picked up before they had traveled much more than an hour. They were getting close when he felt the first drops of rain.

Anny appeared in the companionway. "Can I help?"

"I'll bring her in there," he said, jerking his head toward a sheltered harbor not far away. With luck, he thought he could bring the boat in before the rain began in earnest.

Lady Luck, however, had other ideas. He did manage to get around the spit of land, gain some shelter, drop the sail, and cut the engine. But he didn't make it to the mooring before the rain began pelting down.

Anny, who had gone below once he'd got the sail down and taken the helm again, appeared again, rain streaking down her face, plastering her hair to her head. The T-shirt was gone. So were the shorts. She was wearing two scraps of material and damn all else.

"What the hell are you doing?" he demanded.

She started to climb up toward the bow. "What I do every night." She gestured toward where she always stood and tied the mooring line.

"Like that? In a bikini?"

"The clothes were wet and hard to move in. And it's not cold, even though it's raining. Besides a bikini is easier to dry. So this is better."

The hell it was. "I don't want you out there. Too dangerous." The boat was tossing about on the waves. They were getting bigger every moment.

She turned and stared back at him. "So how are we going to anchor?"

"I'll do it."

"And it's not dangerous for you?"

"It's—"

But she didn't wait for his reply. She was scrambling toward the bow and he found himself staring at a very shapely, barely covered royal posterior. He felt an almost overwhelming desire to smack it.

"Damn it, Anny, clip on your harness line!" he shouted at her. Though God knew what she'd clip it to.

"I'm not stupid." Her words floated back to him on the rising wind. His heart caught in his throat as he watched her balancing as the boat tipped and jerked.

"*Anny!*"

Please, God. Ah, there. He breathed as he saw her fumble with the harness and clip on somehow. Then she started giving him hand signals.

His fingers strangling the wheel, Demetrios tried to bring the boat in as close as he could, as quickly as he could, as smoothly as he could, and get her back safe. The boat dipped and leaned. Anny slipped, dropped the line, and he felt his insides somersault as he watched her.

"Come on, Anny!" He wanted her back. Wanted her safe. She crouched, went down on her knees, reaching and—

"Got it!" Her words were thin on the wind.

But then she was up again, and slip-sliding back to him. Demetrios cut the engine and yanked her back into the cockpit. Into his arms.

His heart was slamming against the wall of his chest. "Don't. Ever. Do. That. Again." He clutched her hard, his arms wrapping around her, his knees still shaking at the memory of her out there, teetering, in harm's way. "Promise me."

She twisted to stare up at him, her eyes wide with surprise, rain still streaming down her cheeks. "I'm f-fine." But her voice sounded thready and insubstantial, though it could have been the wind causing it.

"I'm not," he said. "You scared the hell out of me." And he still didn't want to let go of her, though it wasn't only fear of disaster averted that had him holding her now. It was the feel of her in his arms, the rightness of it.

"I'm sorry. But I was fine. Really. Mission accomplished. And it wasn't so hard."

"No. The hard part would have been me telling your father his daughter had drowned." And knowing it was all his fault.

"I wasn't going to drown." She twisted again and he let her go this time because holding her was not a good idea.

She didn't even seem to notice. "I did exactly what I was supposed to do. It had to be done, and you needed to steer. But—" now she paused and beamed at him "—thank you for worrying about me."

"I was worried about *me*," he said gruffly. "Your old man would probably have had me guillotined. Or do it himself."

"Papa is very civilized."

"I wouldn't be," Demetrios muttered under his breath and knew it for the truth. He glared at her standing there in her bikini. The rain was getting colder now, and her nipples were standing up against the thin fabric. "And for God sake, go get dressed!"

Thank God she did, though not without arching her brows and looking at him thoughtfully for a long minute before she left. Thank God she didn't say anything else, either, but just let it ride.

Demetrios did not want to talk. He did not want to deal with the roil of emotions churning inside him. Did not to face the maelstrom of feelings or the woman who was causing them.

Of course he had to follow her below because he could think of no excuse for staying up on deck in the middle of a pounding rain. Fortunately she was in her cabin. He went to his. He would have stayed there all evening, but she tapped on his door an hour later.

"Dinner's ready."

He hauled himself off his bunk, where he'd been trying with no luck at all to focus on his screenplay, and opened the door a few inches. "We ate."

She shrugged. "Fine. If you're not hungry." She was still looking at him speculatively. "I made bruschetta." A pause. "I'm sorry if I scared you."

He muttered under his breath. "Just don't do it again." He came out and sat down at the table. The rain still pounded down, but the wind seemed to have slacked off a bit so the boat didn't heel over quite as much. It didn't bobble and tip constantly. It made the meal easier to serve and to eat. But he wasn't particularly hungry.

He was distracted by what he was thinking, by what he was feeling. By how badly he didn't want to be thinking and feeling any of it.

Anny was making an effort at conversation. He recognized a couple of her "conversation starters." Questions that invited participation, that welcomed a response. She used them when he wasn't cooperating. Next thing you knew she'd be reduced to asking him what he was thinking.

And there was no way he was telling her that.

She'd barely finished her last mouthful when he stood up. "I'll clean up. You go ahead and work."

Her eyes widened. "Work?"

"Aren't you writing a dissertation?"

The eyes widened a fraction more. Then they narrowed and she looked at him the way his mother had when he'd been a particularly fractious child. But unlike his mother, Anny didn't say anything. She dumped her plate in the sink and gave a small shrug. "Well, you know where to find me."

Anny went straight into her cabin and shut the door. Hard.

What was his problem? She could hear him banging plates and silverware in the galley. If he kept that up, he'd break something, she thought, wincing as she heard a particularly loud clank.

Well, if he did, he could buy Theo whatever it was he'd broken. She wasn't going to do it. Whatever was eating him, it wasn't her fault.

She tried not to care. Tried not to think about it. But like all the rest of her waking moments since he'd swept her away from the Ritz that first afternoon, these moments, too, were filled with Demetrios.

A lot of good not going to bed with him had done—because despite her better judgment and best efforts, she'd fallen in love with him. Not the young man from the poster, though he was part of it, too. But the man who'd taken time for the children at the clinic, the man who had told her not to make decisions that would cause her to regret her life, the man who had offered her refuge on his boat, who made her laugh and made her wistful, who had one night made beautiful love to her, who had been frightened for her. Who had held her in his arms.

Who hadn't kissed her, she reminded herself.

No, he'd held her tight, reassured himself that she was fine, then abruptly let her go. Because he cared. She couldn't say he didn't care. But he wasn't in love with her the way she was with him.

The clanking and clattering in the galley finally ceased. The cabinet door banged shut one last time. Then she heard the door to Demetrios's cabin open and close. And then silence—except for the wind and the rain.

Anny started to reach for her laptop, told herself she might as well work. He was right that she did have her dissertation to do. And it was a part of her future even if he wasn't.

And then she heard the door to his cabin again, then his feet on the companionway stairs heading to the cockpit. Probably checking everything one last time before he battened down for the night.

The splash surprised her.

The boat dipped and it sounded as if he'd thrown something overboard. But what? And why?

It was dark so Anny had to turn off the light to peer out the porthole. At first she couldn't see anything except the lights of the village beyond the harbor and the streaks of reflections across the water.

And then, suddenly, rising out of the water she saw the silhouette of a man's head.

She pressed her nose against the porthole, disbelieving. Then she turned, jerked open the door and pounded up the steps. "Demetrios!"

She reached the cockpit and scrambled over the side onto the deck. "*Demetrios!*"

She scanned the choppy dark sea desperately. What had possessed him to come up on deck? And what had he been doing to fall overboard? He'd been the one worried about her and now—

"Demetrios!" She spotted him now. He was a good twenty yards off the starboard bow and against the streaky reflections she could see his arms stroking in quick rhythm as he cut through the water.

Swimming! *Away* from the boat!

"Demetrios!" Princesses didn't yell. Anny had never bellowed so loudly in her life. "*Demetrios!*"

This time he heard. And slowly, almost reluctantly, it seemed, he turned toward her, treading water. He flicked his hair back off his forehead and slowing, lazily began stroking back toward the boat. "What?" There was a note of annoyance in his voice.

He was annoyed? She thought he'd fallen overboard! And he'd dived in on purpose?

She leaned her forearms on the railing and glared down at him, furious. *"What the hell are you doing?"*

He was beside the boat now, his hair plastered to his skull, droplets glistening against the stubble on his jaw. He looked up at her but he made no move to climb aboard. "Taking a swim," he said, as if it were the most logical thing in the world.

"Now? After dark? Alone? In this weather?" Her voice was shrill. She couldn't help it.

"I felt like some exercise."

"You should have said so," she said through her teeth. "I'd have come with you."

He muttered something she didn't hear.

"What if you'd drowned?" she demanded.

"I wouldn't have drowned." He sounded sure of it. "I've been swimming all my life."

"Then you should know that you shouldn't swim alone! Especially in the dark."

"I was fine."

"I was fine on the bow tonight," she reminded. "You got angry then." She narrowed her gaze down at him as he trod water beside the boat. "Is this payback?"

"What? No. Of course not." He looked indignant.

"Then what is it?"

He didn't answer. Instead he turned and started to swim parallel to the boat as if he were going to continue on past it.

"Swim away and I'm coming after you," Anny warned.

He turned back. "You jump in and I'll drown *you*." There was a level of fury in his tone that didn't make sense to her. The whole stupid episode didn't make sense. But he was a man—that probably explained everything.

"Fine," she said. "If you're so desperate to swim, go right ahead. I'll just sit right here and watch."

"What? And play lifeguard?" He gave her an exasperated look. "Going to hold the life preserver?"

She shrugged. "Why not? I won't say a thing, and I'll only throw it to you if you start to drown." She gave him a saccharine smile.

"Oh, for God's sake!" He took three strokes, reached the side of the boat, then hauled himself up and over the side. Water streamed off his bare legs and dripped from the hems of his shorts. He glared down at her, then shook himself like a dog, showering her with more water than the sky was presently providing.

"Happy now?" he snarled.

Anny stared at his hard muscled body and could barely find the spit to get a single word out of her mouth. "I—"

But Demetrios didn't wait to hear her answer. He vaulted over the side into the cockpit and pounded down the steps to the cabin without another word.

When she dared to follow him a few minutes later, he was already in his cabin. The door was shut. The shower running.

A while later she heard it shut off. There were a few more noises, a cabinet door banging.

Then silence.

Silence as long as she stood there, listening.

"Demetrios?" Her voice came, soft but firm, from the other side of the door. "We need to talk."

No, that was the last thing they needed to do. "Go to sleep," he called.

"I can't."

"Well, I'm going to sleep." He flipped off the light, rolled onto his face, and pulled the sheet over him.

She knocked again. And again.

"Damn it, princess!"

"Please."

The perennially polite royal. Damn it. Demetrios rolled over again, then scrubbed his hands against his hair. "Hang on."

He flicked on the light again, dragged on a pair of boxers and some shorts, pulled a T-shirt over his head, then sucked in a deep and, he hoped, sustaining breath, and cracked open the door.

"What?"

She was looking at him the way she'd looked that night on Gerard's yacht. Worried. Bewildered. Almost as if she was in pain. The last thing he wanted now was a woman in pain.

"I'm confused," she said with her best finishing school eloquence. "And I was hoping you'd enlighten me."

"I'm not very enlightening, princess," he said roughly. "And I don't have a clue what you're talking about. I wanted a swim. I needed some exercise. I'm safe and back on board. So could we maybe do this tomorrow and—" He started to shut the door.

She put her foot in it.

They both looked down at her bare toes. Nails painted a delicate peach color. After a moment, she wiggled them experimentally, then looked at him again. Waiting. Foot not moving.

Demetrios sighed heavily. Then he turned her around and put a hand against her back, moving her out into the main cabin where he pointed her to a chair and sat down opposite. "What do you want to know, princess? On what subject am I supposed to 'enlighten' you?"

She leaned toward him. "Why are you angry at me?"

"I'm not angry at you."

"You're angry at someone."

"No."

But she clearly wasn't buying that. "Not me, then. Yourself?" she ventured. "For letting me come along?"

"No. Yes. Hell, this isn't twenty questions."

"Until you start volunteering something, it will be. We were getting along very well. And now we're not. So what's wrong?"

He narrowed his gaze at her. "Why? Do you think you can fix it?"

"If you won't tell me, we won't know, will we?"

He scowled, then ground his teeth in the face of her gentle, curious, bloody innocent smile. He shoved himself out of his chair, paced the length of the galley, then spun around and snarled, "It's elementary biology, princess."

Her eyes widened. She stared. "It is not."

He blinked, momentarily nonplussed at her denial. "Of course it is. Men. Women. Desire. Surely you remember propositioning me the night we met."

"Yes, and you argued vehemently against it," she replied, color high in her cheeks.

"But apparently not hard enough," he said with a sardonic smile. "Because we had sex."

She opened her mouth, and he wondered if she was going to correct him, use the words she'd used at the time: make love. But she didn't. She said, "And it so thrilled you that you didn't care if we ever did it again."

Now it was his turn to stare. "What?"

"You said it was up to me," she reminded him.

"Because I wasn't making it a condition for you coming along. I said I'd be glad to do it anytime! Just say when, remember?" He arched a brow at her.

She shrugged, then stood up and met his gaze. "Fine," she said. "Let's do it."

He stopped dead still. Couldn't believe his ears. "What did you say?"

She lifted her royal chin. "I said, let's do it." Her gaze was unblinking, her stance defiant.

He felt instantly wary. "You said you needed to protect yourself," he told her, doing his best to reconstruct her argument.

She gave a negligent lift of one shoulder. "Didn't work."

He braced a hand on the galley cabinet. "What do you mean, it didn't work?"

"I fell in love with you, anyway."

He felt as if she'd punched him in the gut. His knees felt weak. Slowly, dazedly, he shook his head. "No, you haven't."

"Clairvoyant, are you?"

"Damn it, Anny. You can't."

"I tried not to," she agreed. "Didn't work. My problem. Not yours. So—" she held out a hand toward him "—shall we?"

He couldn't move. Felt as if he had a rock the size of

Gibraltar stuck in his throat. He took a deep breath. Then another. And another.

"No," he said.

They stared at each other then. Her blue eyes were wide and disbelieving. He didn't blame her. He wasn't sure he believed himself.

"You want me," she said, but she didn't sound entirely convinced.

"Wanting and doing something about it are two different things," he told her in no uncertain terms. He leaned back and folded his arms across his chest. He didn't say a word. He didn't have to.

Outside the rain continued to pelt down. But the wind had slackened. The boat barely rocked.

"I don't understand," she said after a long moment.

"It isn't going to happen."

"You're never going to have sex again?" She cocked her head. "Or you're never going to have sex with me?"

His teeth came together with a snap. Then he said bluntly, "Not with you."

Her lashes fluttered and she shook her head as if he made no sense. "Why?"

He began pacing again. "Simple. You want love. You want marriage. I don't."

"I'm not proposing, just propositioning you. But since you brought up the subject of marriage, why are you so against it?"

His fingers curled into fists. "It's none of your business."

She was quiet a long moment. And then she drew a breath slowly, let it out and said, "Because of Lissa."

He jerked, his gaze sharpening at her words.

"I understand," she said softly. "But you can't mourn her forever, Demetrios. You can't die just because she did. I know you loved her and she loved you. But someday you may love someone else and—"

"She didn't love me," he snapped.

Her fingers knotted in her lap. She looked at him with worried eyes.

"My marriage was a disaster," he told her baldly and saw her eyes widen in shock. "It was the worst thing that I ever did. I made the biggest mistake of my life. It gutted me. And I'm never doing it again. Ever."

She didn't move for an age, and then almost in slow motion she sat up straighter and looked at him, her eyes gentle, warm, compassionate. All the things he didn't need—or want.

"I thought… The magazines said," she corrected herself, "that it was wonderful. You were perfect for each other. She was beautiful."

He leaned a hip against the table and folded his arms across his chest. "I thought so, too. Once," he allowed. "It wasn't like that. She wasn't. Not inside. Not where it matters."

He didn't want to talk about it. Did not want to force himself to relive his marriage to Lissa. He'd already been through it on his own too many times—hundreds of them, maybe thousands, each time an attempt to identify where he could have done something, fixed something, said something to make a difference.

"She was driven. She wanted to be the best. To have the best. That's what mattered. The good films. The good roles. The right house. The right man." He grimaced. "It was all a role in the end. One she'd set her heart on since she was a kid. She had to prove herself."

"Like me," Anny said softly. "Needing to be someone besides a princess."

"Not at all like you," he protested. He flung himself down into the chair beside hers. "You're finding out who you are. But you're not stepping on anyone else in the process. You don't use up and spit out."

She pressed her lips together, but didn't speak. Just listened. And Demetrios, once started, couldn't seem to stop talking.

He told her about the whirlwind courtship, the sense of having found the perfect person to complement who he was. "She played a role. She was—for a time—who I wanted her to be, the love of my life, the woman who was going to bear my children." His jaw tightened. He felt Anny's knuckles rub his knee, was conscious of her touch and grateful for it.

"She used people to get what she wanted, where she wanted," he went on heavily. "I was a stepping-stone on the way. Even when I began to realize things weren't the way I thought they'd be, I believed I could change it. I thought I could make her happy. I thought if we had a family, she'd settle down, be happy." His mouth twisted in rueful recognition of his own self-delusion. "I don't know if anything ever would have made Lissa happy." And that was God's own truth.

"She might have learned," Anny said. "If you'd had children—"

"No," he said sharply. "She didn't want them. She said she did at first. Lied about it," he corrected himself. "Or hell, maybe she even believed it. I don't know where her roles ended and the lies began. But she didn't want kids. She wanted a career. And nothing or no one was going to stand in her way."

He leaned back in the chair, his legs sprawled, his gaze on the ceiling. He didn't say anything for a long moment. Then he went on tonelessly. "I was finishing a film in South Carolina. Acting. Not directing. She'd just finished one herself, and I wanted her to come with me. I thought once I finished there we could go some place together, try to work things out. Start again. Start a family." He stopped. Swallowed. Looked at Anny.

The corner of her mouth tipped gently. She waited.

"She got offered a role in Thailand. Fantastic part, she said. She couldn't turn it down." He recited it all calmly, trying for resigned detachment. Failing. "Wouldn't turn it down. She went to Thailand before I got home. I could have gone when I finished. But she said she was working too hard. She didn't need distractions. And I didn't hear again until I got the call from the director that she was in the hospital." He stopped.

"From a blood infection?" Anny said.

"Yes."

"How horrible. Such a freaky thing to get." She reached out and caught his hand in hers.

"She got it aborting our child," he heard himself tell her. He'd never told anyone that.

Anny stared at him, her eyes wide with shock and disbelief. She didn't say a word. Her fingers said it for her. They wrapped around his tightly—and hung on.

He chewed on the inside of his cheek as he felt the familiar ache in his throat, the sting behind his eyes. "I didn't even know she'd been pregnant. Not until I got there. Not until she told me it didn't...fit into her plans."

He couldn't mask the aching hollowness now. He could talk about Lissa with a certain amount of detachment. But he couldn't ever quite get past this part of her betrayal without feeling like she'd driven a knife into his guts.

As if to illustrate, a gust of wind shoved the boat sideways. It rocked and pitched. And Demetrios sat, depleted, disconnected—except for his fingers still caught in Anny's hand.

Finally he shrugged without looking at her and sighed. "So now you know."

She still didn't speak for a long moment. Then she said quietly, "Now I know." Neither of them moved. Neither of them spoke.

The silence went on. And on.

She kept on holding his hand, her thumb rubbing against the side of his finger giving closeness, contact, comfort.

But he couldn't take any more than that.

"That's why the answer is no, Anny. Because I'm not using you. I'm not taking. I don't know why you think you love me. And I hope to God you're wrong. When you make love again, you should get it in return. You deserve it. And I haven't got any left."

CHAPTER NINE

NOW YOU KNOW.

Anny kept hearing his voice saying those same three words over and over in her head. She didn't sleep a wink.

The determined detachment followed by the bitter pain in Demetrios's voice would have been enough to keep her awake. But imagining the nightmare that had been his marriage kept her tossing and turning the whole night.

She—like everyone else in the world—had thought Demetrios Savas's self-imposed exile had been to come to terms with the loss of the woman he so deeply loved, a woman he'd lost to a mysterious virulent infection of the blood.

It was tragic, certainly.

How dare the reality be so much worse?

She wanted desperately to go to him, to comfort him, to assuage all the pain and anger in him.

At the same time she knew that nothing she could offer would do that. There were some losses so deep that people were never the same after. There was always the aching speculation about what might have been, the hollowness that couldn't be filled.

But wasn't it possible to go on? She wondered. To relearn the ability to love? A man as deeply devoted to his family, as genuinely interested in others, as kind and caring as he'd been to her had to know what love meant.

The fact that he'd denied himself the pleasure of physical

release because "it wouldn't be fair to her" was, perversely, a kind of love in itself.

But she couldn't tell him that. She couldn't tell him, either, that she didn't need him to be the perfect man he'd seemed in her youthful fantasies. Or the perfect man he seemed to expect himself to be. She'd fallen in love with the man he was now, scars and all. And if those scars were deeper than she'd ever imagined, it didn't mean she loved him less.

If anything she loved him more for overcoming the pain, for fighting his way back to a productive life, a spectacular career, a compassion for others.

It wasn't that he didn't have love for other people, Anny decided. It was that he didn't have any for himself.

For the next four days Demetrios kept to himself. The weather turned fine so there was no reason not to focus on making the fastest time possible. He kept conversation to a minimum, said he didn't have time to go for a swim or while away the evenings talking under the stars.

He had a screenplay to write, he told her. And she had a dissertation. So when he wasn't actually sailing the boat or eating a meal, he shut himself in his cabin.

You'd think she'd get the point.

But Anny acted like he hadn't spilled his guts and told her what a mess his marriage had been. Her smiles still seemed genuine. Her questions about sailing, about fishing, about recipes his mother had made, for heaven's sake, didn't abate. She didn't give him pitying glances, thank God.

But she was still Anny. And she wore his NYU shirt and his shorts too damned much.

He should ask for them back. She had stuff she could wear now. She'd bought that damn bikini and a couple of shirts and other shorts and pants as well, hadn't she? But while she wore them, it seemed to him she wore his NYU shirt more.

As if she were silently declaring a bond between them. As if the shirt was hers. As if he was.

He wasn't, damn it! But the awareness that existed between them still hummed loudly, even though Demetrios assured himself it would go away.

It would, but Anny didn't.

He'd always thought Theo's yacht was a decent size. It had always felt spacious, roomy, enough for a whole family. He was wrong.

The boat was tiny. Cramped. Everywhere he went, there was Anny. Even when he was on deck, alone, there she was, below him somewhere, in the galley making dinner, or working on her dissertation in her cabin.

After four days he couldn't take any more. Nothing made any difference. She'd got under his skin. She made him want things he swore he'd never want again, prayed he'd never be tempted by again.

Not because she flirted or teased or promised anything special. She'd done it simply by being Anny.

So when they sailed into the harbor at the tiny Greek island of St. Isaakios the following afternoon, Demetrios felt as if he'd got an answer to his prayers.

Anny watched with growing amazement as hordes of people gathering on the waterfront of tiny St. Issakios. The tiny Greek island where they had put in for the night was celebrating its namesake's feast day.

She had thought Demetrios would give it a miss. But he seemed keen to go ashore. It was the first thing he'd seemed keen on since the night he'd turned her down. She supposed grimly that it was good that something appealed to him.

But she knew she wasn't being fair. He was a man in pain. But the truth was, she wasn't exactly thriving on all this rejection herself.

So when he'd suggested stopping, she said, "Why not?"

"You don't have to go ashore," he told her.

But she'd had enough of being on a boat with a man who looked away every time she came into view. She wanted noise and bright lights and hordes of people as much as he did.

"I can hardly wait," she told him recklessly and was gratified to see his dark eyebrows raise.

The transformation of what was surely the normally sleepy island home of a few hundred fishermen and their families was well underway by the time they climbed into the inflatable just past dusk. Waiting until dark was the one concession they made to the desire for anonymity.

When they finally got ashore, Anny found she didn't have her "land legs" yet and stumbled as she started up the dock. Luckily Demetrios caught her and set her back on her feet. But just as quickly, he let her go again.

"You don't have to stick with me if you'd rather not," Anny said.

Demetrios looked at the milling crowds of people, half of them already drunk and the other half well on their way in that direction. "Don't be an idiot," he said gruffly. "Come on."

The waterfront was jammed with people. Thousands of tiny fairy lights were strung along the streets near the harbor. The heavy bass from the beach concert made the ground shake under their feet. Hurrying to keep up with him, Anny stumbled again.

This time he caught her and hung on. The crowds were growing thicker and more boisterous as they moved away off the dock and onto the street facing the harbor. The noise was deafening and after all their days on the water, this sea of humanity was overpowering.

"It's insane!" she yelled, jostled by a group of boys running through the square. Hundreds, maybe thousands, of people were singing and dancing and shouting, drinking and yelling and throwing each other into the sea.

"You want to go back to the boat?" he shouted the words in her ear.

Someone on the beach was setting off fireworks. Someone else was shooting bottle rockets. Photographers' flashes were like sparklers, glittering and incessant. Anny shook her head. "No." There would only be solitude on the boat. She didn't want that. "It's amazing," she yelled back. "We don't have anything quite like this in Mont Chamion!"

"Lucky you! Let's find a place to eat."

They walked away from the waterfront and found the crowds and the noise dwindled a bit. When they did find a restaurant with an empty table, Demetrios was in no hurry for once.

He'd bolted his meals with her the past four days. But that was when they'd been alone. Now he seemed quite content to eat slowly and order another beer. He didn't talk about anything personal. She did her best with Madame's "conversation starters," but he was immune to all of them. When he did talk, he talked about ideas for his screenplay or about people he needed to talk to when the trip was over—as if he could hardly wait.

Anny listened. She took her time over her meal, too. She knew that they would be in Santorini tomorrow. This was the end of the road. And if this was all she was going to get of Demetrios Savas in her life, she would hang on to the evening for as long as she could.

She did her best. Even so it seemed no time at all—though it was probably at least a couple of hours—until Demetrios said, "We should get an early start in the morning. I talked to Theo today and he wanted to know what time we'd be in. I figure we can be there by late afternoon." He even smiled, as if he were counting the minutes until he got rid of her.

Anny just nodded and said, "I'm looking forward to meeting your brother."

Demetrios blinked, as if the notion hadn't occurred to him. Was he going to shuffle her off to a hotel before she could even meet Theo?

He didn't say. But abruptly he called for the check and paid for the meal, standing up as if she didn't still have a half a glass of wine in front of her. "We should get going," he said.

The crowds in the streets had dispersed somewhat now, some moving into *tavernas* to get down to some serious drinking, others onto the roofs of local houses where small parties continued.

The main party had moved from the beach to the *agora*—the small open-air market area—which faced the harbor. The loud rock band had dispersed—probably into the *tavernas* or away in boats—and a smaller group playing more traditional music was delighting the crowd. Couples were dancing, arms around each other, moving to the music, to each other. Anny slowed her pace, watching them, envying them.

"Come on." Demetrios caught her hand so they could skirt around the crowd.

But caught by a combination of music and desire, Anny dug in her heels. "Dance with me."

"*What*?" He stopped abruptly, a flicker of annoyance crossing his features. He gave her hand another tug.

Anny didn't move. "Just one dance." She looked at him beseechingly.

His jaw tightened. "Anny—"

But she wouldn't be gainsayed. Not now. "One dance, Demetrios. One."

The musicians weren't great. The music was tinny and sometimes out of tune. It didn't matter. Their trip was almost over. She knew Demetrios wasn't going to wake up and discover that she wasn't Lissa, or anything like her.

She couldn't argue him around to believing that. Just as she couldn't argue him around to loving her.

So she'd take what she could get: one dance.

She wanted to feel his arms around her one more time. Not making love. But loving. Loving him.

Tomorrow or the next day these memories would be all she'd have left to relish, to savor. She looked up at him, her eyes speaking to him.

His mouth twisted. He rubbed a hand over the stubble that was now a reasonably respectable two-week-old beard. If he danced with her she could turn her head, press her cheek to his jaw and feel that beard. She'd only felt it in her imagination until now.

If they danced, she'd have one more memory to sustain her.

"Just a dance, Demetrios. To remember."

He hesitated, then shrugged. "Oh hell. Why not?"

It was hell—and heaven—all rolled into one.

The minute he slipped his arms around Anny to dance with

her, the moment he felt her body fit itself to his, Demetrios knew he was done for.

He would have laughed bitterly at his own foolishness, if the desire for her weren't so intense, if the longing weren't so real. Anger and desperation he could fight.

He couldn't fight this.

It was like having his dreams come true. It was like being offered a taste of all he'd ever longed for. A single spoonful that would have to last him for the rest of his life.

"To remember," Anny had said, like it was a good thing.

How could it be good to have a hollow aching reminder of the joy he'd once believed was his due. It wasn't. He didn't believe in promises anymore. Yet, as much as he tried not to give in, he couldn't resist.

It was like trying to resist gravity. Like agreeing to step off a cliff—then refusing to let himself fall.

Impossible.

He drew her closer, looped his arms around her and rested his cheek against her hair. It was so soft, tendrils like butterfly wings tickled his nose. He breathed in the scent of her—a heady combination of citrus and the sea, and permeating everything something indefinably essentially Anny.

They barely moved as the music played on. They simply held each other, swaying, savoring, dreaming—

The camera flash came like a shot in the dark. Once. Twice. Half a dozen times. Blinding him as it moved in and around them in quick succession.

Not, he realized at once, just aimed at him. Aimed at Anny, too. And the rapid repeat fire speed of the shutter flashes told him it wasn't a tourist's camera. *Paparazzo.*

He swore under his breath as he felt her stiffen in his arms. He drew her close, shielded her. "Are you okay? I'm sorry. I'll get him. I'll stop him!"

But almost instantly she stepped back, looking as stunned as he was, but immediately laying a hand on his arm. "No. It's all right. It happens."

She sounded calm, collected. He was furious. "It'll be in every damn tabloid on the continent. Totally misconstrued."

Lissa had loved that sort of thing, delighted in the notoriety. But he was surprised that Anny wasn't more upset.

"I'll talk to him." She was already looking for the jerk.

"Talk?" Since when did you talk to paparazzi?

But Anny was hurrying after the photographer, calling out in perfect fluent Greek, "Please stop. Come talk to me."

Please? Demetrios rolled his eyes.

But the photographer stopped. Demetrios would have happily grabbed his camera and throttled the man on the spot.

Anny was all charm. "Isn't the festival wonderful?" She smiled at the photographer. "How long have you been here? Did you get lots of good shots? Have you had a good day?"

Her and her bloody "conversation starters"! But it worked. And while Demetrios watched, Anny used an arsenal of charm and camaraderie to disarm and enchant the man who had stolen their privacy.

She didn't take his camera and destroy his pictures. She gave him a story to go with them, explaining that she was getting her Ph.D. in archaeology and did he know about the nearby ruins? She'd always wanted to see them and her dear friend Demetrios, whom she'd chanced to meet up with at the festival in Cannes, had offered to bring her today.

Not a word of it was untrue. She never said they'd actually seen the ruins. She never said she'd spent close to two weeks on a sailboat with him. She said they'd had a wonderful time and a wonderful meal and who could resist dancing after such a wonderful day?

Then she said with an impish smile, "Will you dance with me?"

The photographer almost dropped his teeth.

"I'll hold the camera," Demetrios offered helpfully.

But the photographer was no fool. "Nice try," he laughed. "But even a dance with a princess isn't worth the price of these photos." And giving them a quick salute he hurried away.

"You would have crushed his camera," Anny said flatly.

"Damn straight."

She sighed, then shrugged. "Well, you have your way and I have mine."

"He'll print the pictures."

"Yes. But it won't embarrass my father when he sees them."

Demetrios sat silently with his hand on the tiller of the inflatable's small engine all the way back to Theo's boat. He had closed in on himself in a way that shouldn't have surprised her.

He'd been more and more reclusive since he'd told her about his marriage to Lissa. But this felt different. He didn't seem bitter so much as thoughtful. He was probably upset about the photos, thinking she had been a fool. She didn't think so. Her father had taught her never to be adversarial unless it was absolutely necessary. It hadn't been.

But she felt sad now. Happy she'd been able to defuse the situation with the photographer. But at what cost?

The end of her closeness with Demetrios. The flashes had come like the clock striking midnight in the middle of Cinderella's last dance. And now whenever she remembered their dance, the memory wouldn't be the one she wanted.

But they couldn't go back to the *agora* and recapture it. The photographer had departed happily enough, and she wasn't worried about what he would say in his story. But their anonymity had departed with him.

Now everyone stopped to look at them. To whisper. To stare. To nudge.

"A princess," they whispered. "With Demetrios Savas—he is Greek, you know."

So they'd gone to the dock and came straight back to the boat. She got a rock in her sandal and didn't even stop to shake it out until they were on the boat.

Now, after he'd tied the inflatable onto the stern of the sailboat, Demetrios helped her out, then hauled the inflatable aboard after them.

"Can I help you stow it?" Anny offered, knowing the answer before she even asked the question.

"I can manage." He made quick work of stowing it.

Anny, having lost her chance at the dance, still wouldn't give up on the moment. She sat down on the bench in the cockpit and took off her sandals while she watched Demetrios work.

The sound of the music carried across the water. Sweet hummable, danceable music that made Anny remember the way Demetrios's arms had felt around her, the way his beard had felt against her cheek. Her throat ached. She curled her toes, then relaxed them again, then rubbed the muscles on the sole of her foot.

"Let me."

She looked up, startled, to see Demetrios sit down next to her and pull her foot up onto his lap and begin massaging her instep. She wanted to whimper.

Maybe she did whimper. His fingers were so strong, so firm. So unexpected.

Then he reached down to pick up her other foot, and once more strong fingers kneaded her sole, stroked her toes.

"Better?"

She nodded. Her feet felt boneless. Her body was quivering. Her eyes flickered shut.

"Then dance with me."

Her eyes flew open. She stared. It was almost totally dark. His expression was unreadable. There was a rough edge to his voice.

"No flashbulbs here," he said. "But we can still hear the music." Then he lifted her feet off his lap and stood, holding out his hand to her.

Anny swallowed. Then she stood and went into his arms. She felt them close loosely around her, then tighten, fitting their bodies together. Her lips brushed his beard as she lifted her face. Then he rested his cheek against her hair.

She slid her hands up his back, and relished the feel of the soft cotton and hard muscle under her palms. Her fingers caressed the nape of his neck, kneaded and stroked, then traced the curve of his ear.

It was heaven. Eternity. She memorized every touch, every

movement, the pounding of his heart against hers. She didn't ask why. She only knew joy. Dared to believe.

And then the music stopped.

He didn't step away. He stayed there, stood there, holding her. Then a long while later, when the music began again—something light and lively this time—he lifted his head and she reached up and touched his bearded cheek, lay her palm against it and knew she would never forget the feel.

He took her hand and opened it to kiss the center of her palm.

Anny felt a shiver of longing run through her. "Please," she whispered.

Their gazes locked, held.

A sound caught in his throat. And then he took her and drew her toward the stairs.

Maybe it was because she didn't use the word *love*.

Maybe it was because he was at the end of his rope.

Maybe—and this was what she dared hope for most of all— he finally believed in the love she felt for him and was learning he loved her in return.

He never said. She didn't ask.

It was enough tonight to simply show him. No past, no future—only now.

They were kissing again before they got down the companionway steps. She nearly fell on top of him.

"Careful." He caught her and began undressing her.

They barely made it to her cabin. He scooped her up and laid her on her bunk, then came down beside her, his hands tugging her shirt over her head as hers did the same to his.

She raked her fingers over the soft, yet wiry, hair on his chest, even as he cupped her breasts and bent to kiss them through the lace of her bra. But it wasn't enough. His fingers fumbled for only a moment with the clasp, and then he had it off and was kissing her there again.

She grabbed his hair in her fists and tugged. He lifted his head to say, "You don't like that?"

"I like it. I—" She shifted, unable to say what she wanted, what she liked. "It makes me…want more."

And he promised, "There will be more."

He kissed her again, down the center of her chest, then each breast in turn. He laved them, teased them, made her nipples peak and her body move restlessly on the bunk.

And then he was skimming the rest of their clothes off and stroking her, starting at her feet, kissing her knees, letting his fingers wander up her thighs.

Anny bit her lip, trembling at the sensations he caused. But it wasn't only the sensations, it was the man. It was Demetrios she loved. And her own fingers reached to touch him, to trace their way down his belly, following the line of dark hair to the core of his masculinity.

She ran her fingers through the thatch of dark hair at the juncture of his thighs, trailed the tip of one finger along the length of him. He sucked in a sharp breath.

"Anny!"

"What?"

But then his fingers found her, too, dipped in and caressed her, and she didn't need to ask "what" anymore. She knew. She shivered and pressed against his fingers.

Then he nudged her knees apart and settled between them. He loomed over her, his eyes hooded, the skin taut across his cheekbones, his face more beautiful now than she had ever seen it.

She touched him again, stroked him. Learned the shape and hot silken texture of him. She hadn't dared do this last time. She barely dared now. And as soon as she had, she wanted to do it again. And again.

A breath hissed between his teeth. "Anny."

"Yes," she said.

"Now," she said.

"Please," she said.

At that, a sudden laugh caught in his throat. And then he slid into her. Her own breath caught.

Perfect. Union.

His eyelids fluttered. His head tipped back, the chords of his neck stood out. For a long moment he held himself perfectly still. And then he began to move.

And Anny moved with him. Rocked him. Held him.

And the two of them shattered together. Their solitary beings broken, splintered by their climax.

But as she ran her fingers lightly down his sweat-slicked back, in her heart Anny made them whole together in her love.

CHAPTER TEN

THEY WERE ALREADY underway the next morning by the time Anny awoke.

That had never happened before. She'd always awakened the moment the engine started. Not this morning.

But she'd never before had a night like last night, either. She rolled over in Demetrios's bed, feeling more amazing than she'd ever felt in her life. He was gone, of course. The sheet was cool. So was the pillow. He hadn't stayed, but it didn't matter—because he loved her.

When you make love again, you should get it in return. You deserve it. He had said those words to her. He wouldn't have done it if he hadn't.

She reached for his pillow, picked it up and brought it against her face, drawing in a deep breath and, with it, the subtle scent of him—sea and salt, a faint hint of some sort of balsam shampoo, and something essentially Demetrios.

She hugged the pillow to her as she'd held him last night, wrapping her arms around it, clinging as if she would never let go. Of course she had. And he had gone.

But he loved her. She knew it.

She got up and took a shower, long and leisurely, discovering as she did so that her body felt different now. Muscles she had barely known she had were a little sore, a delicious reminder of her night of love with Demetrios.

She washed her hair, combed it long and straight, then dressed in a pair of her own new shorts, but chose to wear Demetrios's NYU T-shirt with it. It was hers.

And she was his.

She took her time, savoring the moments, making breakfast for the two of them before she took the eggs and ham up to him. She felt fresh and loved and yet oddly self-conscious as she climbed the stairs and smiled at him.

He saw her the instant she appeared. There was no answering smile.

He said, "I'm sorry."

Anny stiffened, felt as if she'd been slapped. "*Sorry*? You didn't like it?"

"Of course I liked it. It was…amazing. But…I'm sorry it happened. It shouldn't have."

Stung, tears springing to her eyes and blinking rapidly because she was damned if she was going to cry, she retorted. "Oh? And do you say that to all the girls?"

Demetrios's knuckles went white on the wheel. "No, damn it, I don't. Because ordinarily I don't make mistakes like that."

"You married Lissa."

He jerked as if she'd slapped him.

"I'm sorry," she said quickly. Then retracted the apology at once. "No, I'm not. I'm sorry you had a bad marriage. I'm sorry she hurt you. I'm sorry—beyond sorry—she aborted your child and destroyed your dreams. I'm sorry she's dead. But I am not Lissa!"

"No," he said roughly. "You aren't. You're worth a thousand of her. You're worth a thousand of me. You deserve a whole hell of a lot better than what happened between us last night."

"Thank you very much," she said tightly. "Not."

"Hell, Anny." He raked a hand through his hair. "See? That's why it was a mistake. You care!"

"So do you!"

"No."

"Liar. You said when I made love next I deserved to get it in return. I got it last night."

His jaw clenched. He looked away, shaking his head, then finally back at her. "I care about you, yes," he allowed.

"Big of you," she muttered.

"Which is exactly why it was wrong. I was wrong. I was…caught up in the moment. God, that sounds asinine. I wanted a memory, too! But I shouldn't have done it. I shouldn't have raised your expectations. I shouldn't have—"

"Oh, you raised my expectations, did you? Did you think I was coming up here to propose marriage this morning?"

A harsh line of red lit his cheekbones. "I hope not," he said flatly. "Because while it was wrong, it doesn't change anything."

It changed everything. He just didn't know it yet. But she didn't say it. This wasn't something she could convince him of by argument. He had to come to know it in his gut the same way she did.

He had further to go. She needed to give him time.

"I love you, Demetrios."

He flinched at her words. His teeth came together and he shook his head. "Don't."

She smiled through her pain. "Too late now."

"It's not," he insisted.

"Yes," she said firmly. "It is."

And that was the absolute truth.

They reached Santorini late that afternoon.

A man instantly identifiable as a Savas was waiting at the dock. She knew Demetrios had radioed Theo to say what time they would be arriving. It was obvious he hadn't bothered to say that he wasn't alone.

Theo's curiosity was instant and obvious. Demetrios was determinedly offhand. "This is Anny. Anny, my brother Theo. Anny lives in Cannes. She's a doctoral student, working on her dissertation. She needed a break for a couple of weeks, so she came along to crew for me."

Theo grinned. He took Anny's hand in his big callused one

and gave it a squeeze. "Doctoral student, huh? Impressive. Smart and beautiful. Little brother's taste is improving."

Demetrios looked up sharply from the line he was stowing. "She's not—"

Theo lifted a brow. "Not smart? Not beautiful? Not single?" he challenged.

Anny couldn't help but laugh.

Demetrios's teeth came together with a snap. He stood up abruptly. "Don't just stand there. Get my gear and I'll take Anny's. She'll be staying at Lucio's."

"Ma won't hear of it."

"*Ma* won't—" Demetrios stopped dead and turned his head to stare narrowly at his brother. "Ma's not here. Theo, tell me she's not here."

Theo shrugged helplessly "What can you do? It's their house."

Demetrios muttered something under his breath. For a moment Anny thought he might balk, leave her there and head straight back out to sea. He seemed to be considering his options. Theo gave Anny a conspiratorial look, but just waited patiently.

Finally Demetrios sighed and rubbed a hand over his face. "You knew," he accused his brother.

"I didn't, actually. Martha might have," he allowed. "Ma works in mysterious ways. And, let's face it, she wants to see you."

Demetrios appeared to grind his teeth. Then he nodded. "Right. Let's get it over with."

The Savas house, which had originally belonged to Theo's wife Martha's family, and was now shared by both extended families, had been expanded by their taking over houses on both sides.

"Room for everyone," Theo told her as he tossed their duffel bags into his car. He gestured up the steep hillside overlooking the town of Thira. "It's a great place. Best thing the old man ever won."

Anny gave him a quizzical look. "Won?"

So while he drove them up the narrow winding road, Theo regaled her with the tale of the sailboat race that he, in fact—not his father—had won against Aeolus Antonides. It was a tale of golf games and sailboat races and in the end it had garnered them a share of the lovely old house. "And my wife," Theo said. "And Tallie's husband."

Anny's eyes widened. She'd only heard of these people. Demetrios had talked about his family growing up. He'd not been very forthcoming about more recent years. But there was no time to ask now because as Theo finished, he was pulling to a stop in front of the walled steps leading up to the house.

"Come on, then, prodigal son," Theo said cheerfully, giving his brother a cuff on the shoulder before he opened the door.

Truer words were never spoken, Anny thought as she watched from the backseat. For the minute Theo opened his car door, the gate to the walled stairway banged open and a veritable horde of people of all sizes and ages hurtled out onto the pavement.

A pretty young dark-haired woman grabbed Demetrios before he could even get out of the car. An older man who must have been his father did pull him out, and he was immediately wrapped in the arms of a woman who could only be Demetrios's mother. She was talking and laughing and crying all at the same time.

Demetrios looked stunned. He moved stiffly at first, but then his arms came up and wrapped hard around his mother and his father as well. He bent his head, kissed them both. And then he was completely enveloped by all of them, then swept up the stairs, leaving her in silence.

Theo opened the car door for her and offered her a lopsided grin. "They do the prodigal thing pretty well, don't they?"

Anny swallowed the lump in her throat. "They do. And they should. It's wonderful to see how much you all love him."

"We do," Theo agreed. He banged the car door shut. "Though he's made it damn difficult these last few years." He opened the boot and got out their duffel bags. "The folks haven't seen him since Lissa's funeral," he told her. "No one in the family has except me. And I did because I turned up on his doorstep once without warning and he couldn't pretend he wasn't home." He dropped their luggage on the pavement, then slammed the lid. "She has a lot to answer for, that woman."

Anny was surprised. "You know about Lissa?" She didn't think from what Demetrios said, he'd told anyone.

Theo snorted and confirmed it. "Not from him. He wouldn't say a word. But I know my brother. I know what he's like—what he *was* like," he corrected himself. "She wasn't good for him. She changed him. I'm sorry she's dead," he said gruffly. "But I'm not sorry she's out of his life."

Which pretty much summed up her own feelings, Anny thought.

"It's a relief to see him with you, let me tell you." Theo held open the gate to the stairs for her and she passed gratefully from the blistering heat of the midday sun to the relative coolness of the trellised bougainvillea-shaded stairs that wound upwards toward the house.

"He's not— We're not…together," Anny felt compelled to say, however much she wished it weren't true.

Theo stopped and narrowed his gaze at her. "No? Who says? Him? Or you?"

Anny couldn't help smiling at how well Theo had assessed the situation. "Demetrios."

A grin slashed across Theo's tanned face. "Ah, well. As long as you don't say it."

Anny didn't say anything at all because they had reached the front door, which stood open to a wide entryway leading to an open living room full of the same jumble of people. She didn't see Demetrios.

"Ma will be feeding him," Theo said. "Come on and meet the family. There won't be a quiz at the end or anything, so relax. They don't bite."

He took her from group to group and introduced her to their sister Tallie, who turned out to be the young woman who had opened the car door, her husband Elias, and their children, another brother, Yiannis, who was arguing with a guy called Lukas who might have been Elias's brother, but Anny wasn't sure.

She met Martha, Theo's wife, who kissed both her cheeks and said, "Have we met? You look familiar?" She seemed to be studying Anny closely.

Quickly Anny shook her head. "No. I haven't met any of Demetrios's family."

Martha laughed. "Lucky you. But then, we're glad to have you. And if you survive all the Savases and the Antonideses, we'll know you deserve him. Good luck."

So it seemed that more than just Theo thought they were "together." Anny was pleased, though she didn't imagine Demetrios would be.

"He's a good man, Demetrios," Martha said. "Almost as good as this one," she said, slipping her arm around Theo's waist.

Anny envied them their obvious love, their easy closeness. She saw the same thing again between Tallie and Elias. He had one of their twins on his shoulders and the other hanging off one arm, but his free arm was around his wife as he talked to Yiannis and Lukas. The joy of connection—of a relationship based on true love and commitment—was so clear. So obvious.

Anny wanted it so badly. With Demetrios.

She wondered if her yearning showed on her face for Theo said suddenly, "Come on out to the kitchen. You need to meet the folks."

Malena and Socrates Savas welcomed her with open arms and profound apologies.

"We didn't realize Demetrios was bringing a guest," his mother said. "We are so happy to meet you. So glad he brought you. Where are you from? Who are your parents?"

"She's a friend, Ma," Demetrios cut in before she could reply. "She crewed for me. That's all."

Malena raised a brow, then said. "Of course, dear." But it didn't stop her from studying Anny closely, then nodding and patting her cheek. "You have done him good."

"Ma!"

Malena ignored him. "Come." She steered Anny to a chair in the kitchen. "Sit down. Eat."

The rest of the afternoon was a whirlwind of activity—of siblings and in-laws, nephews and nieces, all of them eager to welcome Demetrios home again.

"It's a madhouse," he muttered at one point when he came to stand beside her. "I'm sorry."

Anny wasn't. "I love it. You are so lucky to have them. All of them. Such a wonderful family. You are blessed."

He grunted a reply. But she knew he agreed. She'd heard that love those evenings when he'd talked to her about his family. He had missed them. He just needed to figure out how to fit back into the family group.

They made it easy for him. His parents were, of course, thrilled that he was finally home. His sister and brothers—they were all there except George—never mentioned the past three years. They just caught him up on what was going on. They drew him back into the fold as if he'd never been away. The in-laws were equally welcoming. The oldest nephews, Tallie's twins, Nick and Garrett, and Theo's Edward had seen videos of Luke St. Angier. They even remembered him as a favorite uncle from the pre-Lissa days. And it didn't take them long to warm up to him again, to climb all over him and drag him into their games. And while sometimes he looked briefly lost and hollow-eyed, they won him over.

They won Anny over, too. And she won them because she knew the games that little boys played. She told them all about Alex and Raoul and David and said how much her brothers would love to play with this roughhousing clan.

"Go get 'em," Edward suggested. "Bring 'em here."

Anny laughed. "I'd love to, but they live a long way away."

"Take a plane," Nick advised.

"Or a limo," Garrett said, making car noises.

"Limos don't go fast," his brother argued.

"Do so!"

"Do not!"

The discussion that followed didn't require any help from Anny at all.

Nothing much required her help for the rest of the day and evening. But she never felt left out. They made her feel a part of their family. And of course she wasn't allowed to go to Lucio's.

"It's crazy here, Ma. She doesn't need to put up with this," Demetrios argued.

Malena straightened up and gave a sharp look. "This is our home. We want her here. She is welcome here. You will stay, Anny?"

Demetrios wanted her to go, she could see it on his face. But Anny was determined to take what she could get.

"I would love to stay, Mrs. Savas."

Demetrios's mother beamed and wrapped her in a warm hug. "Malena, dear. You must call me Malena."

She spent the night in the room right across the hall from him. Shared it with his three-year-old niece, Caroline, for God's sake. She didn't seem to mind a bit when his mother suggested it.

"At Lucio's she'd have a room of her own," he'd pointed out.

But no one listened to anything he said. Just like old times, he thought.

But it was painful to watch her with them. She was so obviously delighted to be part of things. They were falling all over themselves to bring her into the fold, and nothing he could say or do seemed to have any effect at all.

The next morning she and Caroline appeared together in the doorway to the breakfast room, holding hands.

"Ah. Did you sleep well, my Anny?" his mother asked.

Her Anny! His teeth ground together. He took a gulp of coffee and nearly scalded his throat.

"Come." His mother was making a place for her at the table across from him, between Yiannis and one of the babies in a high chair. "Sit. We have yogurt, fresh fruit. Eggs, ham. Martha is making French toast. Do you like French toast?"

"I love it," Anny said and, as usual, offered to help.

Next thing he knew she was eating a yogurt with one hand, feeding the baby next to her, and talking to his sister, Tallie, about Viennese pastries at the same time. Her gaze lit on him regularly. He watched her while trying not to. But he was weak where she was concerned. He couldn't help it.

And seeing the woman he loved—yes, all right, he loved

her!—happily involved with his family was a scene he'd always dreamed of. He'd cast Lissa in that role and knew very quickly the mistake he'd made. He wasn't going to make another one. And he wasn't going to let Anny make one. But watching Anny take a cloth and wipe the baby's mouth, then offer her another spoonful of cereal, was a sight that made him ache.

Suddenly the door to the roof garden banged open and Edward hurtled into the room. "Daddy! There's a limo coming up the hill."

"It's stoppin' right out front!" Nick and Garrett came roaring in on his heels.

Abruptly, Theo, Yiannis, Lukas and Socrates hurried up the stairs to have a look. Demetrios didn't move. Anny went suddenly still.

His mother paused, putting eggs on a plate. "A limo? For you, Demetrios? Not already," she said.

He shook his head. "Not for me." But he knew who it was for. "It's for Anny."

Anny knew who the limo was for the moment Edward said the word.

The jig is up, she thought. *The fairy tale is over. The photos had reached the palace.*

And yet, at the same time, she didn't believe it. She was a princess wasn't she? Princesses got happy endings—especially if they risked for them. It was the essence of good storytelling.

Besides, Demetrios loved her.

Anny knew it. She could see it in his eyes when he watched her. And even when he pretended he wasn't watching, she knew better. Wherever he was in the room, she could feel his gaze on her.

Now she looked at him and smiled tentatively, but determinedly. Prayed that he would smile back. That he would own up to his feelings, accept them, act on them. Love her.

Of course there would have to be explanations. Anny knew that. His family would have to be told. She dabbed at the baby's sweet face once more, making sure it was clean, then pasted on her best public smile and prepared to make them.

But abruptly Demetrios said, "Anny's not just Anny, Ma. She's Her Royal Highness, Princess Adriana of Mont Chamion."

For a split second Malena Savas looked at her middle son as if he were speaking a foreign language. Uncomprehending. Then, as the truth dawned, her face registered shock. Then, abruptly, resolution. In the next instant, she was wiping her hands on a towel and saying briskly, "Go get your father, Tallie. And tell him to tuck his shirt in."

Anny wanted to say it didn't matter. Nothing mattered but this—she and Demetrios. Being part of his family. Forever.

She looked at Demetrios.

He straightened almost imperceptibly. "I'll get the door."

Her father hadn't sent his driver. He hadn't sent his minister.

When Demetrios came back a few moments later and opened the door to allow the newcomer to precede him, Anny discovered that her father had come himself.

He stood just inside the door, a man of medium height and average build. But you knew he was a king just by looking at him, Anny thought. He had the carriage of generations of royal upbringing. He stood straight under years of responsibility. He had an aura about him of presence, of command. He was in charge and no one doubted it.

Yet in his eyes she saw concern. New lines of worry seemed to crease his face. They softened now at the sight of her. "Adriana."

"Papa." Her voice wobbled for a moment, weighed down by the sudden guilt she felt from having caused those lines, that concern. "You didn't have to come all this way."

"Of course I had to come," he said. "You are my daughter."

"Yes, but—"

"I saw the photos," he said. "I knew who you were with. Where you had to be going. Certainly I had to come." He held out a hand to her then.

Vaguely aware that the room behind her was filling with amazed and intrigued family members, coming back down from the roof garden and tumbling out of the kitchen to stare, Anny crossed the few feet that separated them. She kissed her father on both cheeks and felt the gentle but firm press of his lips on hers as well.

She stepped back, but he didn't let go. He held her away from him and looked into her eyes for a long moment, seeking, searching. And once more she felt a stab of guilt at the same time she knew that she had done the right thing. She couldn't have stayed and married Gerard. She had to make her own way, be true to herself, to love as she would.

Instantly she looked around for Demetrios. He was standing by his father, his expression unreadable. She reached out a hand to him.

"This is Demetrios, Papa," she said.

He stepped forward, but he didn't come and take her hand. He nodded politely to her father. "Your Highness."

"Yes. We met when he answered the door." Her father's gaze settled on Demetrios, looking at him with that same searching look.

Now, Anny thought. *Say it now. Say you love me. Tell him.*

But Demetrios remained silent, meeting her father's gaze implacably.

And so Anny stepped into the breach. Madame would have been proud. "Papa, I'd like you to meet Demetrios's family."

She introduced them all. Malena offered him coffee and biscuits. Socrates inquired about his flight. Garrett, Nick and Edward hopped up and down and finally wanted to know if the limo driver would let them see the inside of it.

Demetrios didn't say a word.

Her father drank a cup of coffee and ate two biscuits. He listened politely when Anny talked about their journey and drew Theo into a discussion of the boat.

Demetrios didn't say a word.

Her father discussed private jets with Socrates, and boat-building with Elias, and he generously allowed the little boys to roam all over the limo and seemed amused when Lukas and Yiannis clattered down the steps to have a look with them. He looked at Demetrios.

Demetrios didn't say a word.

Anny willed him to speak. Willed him to come to her, to hold out a hand to her and admit his love. She didn't see or even feel his gaze upon her though she stared at him nearly every moment. He was in the room, but he seemed to have withdrawn completely.

Finally her father declined another cup of coffee, said, "No, thank you very much," politely to the offer of more biscuits, and stood up. Instantly every man and woman in the room stood up, too.

"If you will collect your things, my dear. We should go."

Go. Leave her dream. Go back to the real world. Anny held her breath, wishing on all the stars in the universe as she looked across the room at the man of her dreams, her heart in her eyes.

"I'll get her bags," Demetrios said.

CHAPTER ELEVEN

DEMETRIOS couldn't stand there and watch her go.

He got her bags from her room and carried them down to the car, aware of what seemed like hordes of his relatives pressing around Anny and her father, following them to the limo. He couldn't do that.

So he said goodbye the only way he could. He went up to the rooftop garden and looked down to watch her embrace his parents, his sister, his brothers, all the children. Then she looked around.

For him? He knew the answer to that. Of course she was looking for him—because she loved him. As, God help him, he loved her.

He had fallen in love a little bit when she'd let him sweep her off her feet. She'd been a good sport when he needed one. And when he'd seen her with Franck and the other kids at the clinic, giving of herself, doing what needed to be done, he'd fallen a bit more. He'd fallen a little deeper that night on Gerard's yacht, when he realized how far she'd been prepared to go—to marry for her country, not for herself. Loyalty and devotion were so much a part of who Anny was.

It was none of his business, of course, but he knew he couldn't let her do it. Though how he would have stopped her, he didn't know. Thoughts of breaking up a royal wedding to save her from herself were a bit over-the-top—but not by much.

But how could he let her tie herself to a loveless marriage?

He knew about loveless marriages. Knew the aching loneliness, the sense of failure. Gerard wasn't Lissa, of course. But Anny deserved so much more.

So when he was tempted to hurtle down the stairs and say, "Don't go," he didn't. His knuckles tightened on the waist-high white-washed wall, anchoring him right where he was.

Then the chauffeur helped her in. Her father joined her. And the limo pulled away. The glass was tinted. He couldn't see past it, couldn't see Anny now. But he didn't need to see her to know how she looked.

She was there on the inside of his eyelids when he closed them. She was there in his dreams when he slept. She was a part of every fiber of his being.

She'd said he loved her, and truer words were never spoken. But what did he have to offer a woman like Anny?

He had made it back from the disaster that had been his marriage to Lissa. But he wasn't the man he had been. He had nothing to give her except what he'd given her these past two weeks—the chance to be herself without the demands of her country and her title, the chance to discover what she wanted, who she was.

He knew who he was.

He also knew she didn't need a man like him. He had too much baggage. Too many bad memories. Too little belief in happy endings.

And more than anyone he knew, Anny deserved a happy ending.

At least he had memories, thanks to her. It was ironic, he supposed, that she'd been the one to ask him for a memory that first night. He'd never imagined how much it would matter to him that he had it, too. And he had memories of these past two weeks with her as well. Memories of her laughter, her joy, her hard work, her generosity, memories of the most lively, loving woman he would ever meet.

And last night. He would never forget last night—never forget making love to her one last time. He shouldn't have done it, should have resisted.

But how could anyone resist when Anny said, *please*?

Thank God she hadn't looked at him a few minutes ago and said, *Please. Please ask me to stay. Please don't let me go.*

If she had, there was no way he could have let her go back to her real life, to her kingdom, to whichever prince she would ultimately marry. To a future without him. He only managed to because he loved her. And because he'd come up here alone.

He couldn't have stood there among his family and watched her leave. Couldn't have smiled and said all those polite things Anny knew how to say. Couldn't have kissed her cheeks and wished her happy because he knew it was the right thing to do, because he knew she would be better off without him.

He might have three Emmy nominations, a Golden Globe and fifteen films under his belt, but he wasn't that good an actor.

They had barely left the Savas family behind when Papa spoke. "I have spoken to Gerard."

Anny jerked. "I'm not—" she began.

But her father shushed her and took her hand in his. "You are not marrying him," he said in his gentle but firm voice. "Yes, I know."

"I'm sorry, Papa. I know you want me to. But I can't!"

"My Anny." Her father chafed her fingers with his, all the while regarding her gravely with his deep brown eyes. "I only ever wanted you to be happy." A rueful look flickered across his face. "And I hoped…" He shrugged. "Gerard is a good man. Older, yes, but not doddering like me."

"You're not doddering!"

"Perhaps not. But foolish I could be. The point is, I thought it would be a good marriage, a marriage like mine and your mother's. That you might grow to love each other as we did. Our marriage was arranged, too, you know."

"Yes," Anny said quietly. But she'd always believed her parents had been in love before their marriage. She'd blinked in surprise at her father's revelation. And then she'd said, "I'm glad it happened for you. But I can't!"

He nodded. "I know. I knew it when I saw the pictures."

The pictures.

He picked up a folder from the seat and opened it, handing her a stack of photos, and the tabloids that had printed them. And seeing them, Anny knew they were easily worth a thousand words apiece, those pictures the paparazzo had taken on St. Isaakios.

There were half a dozen at least of the two of them dancing. She and Demetrios had their arms locked around each other, their bodies in tune with each other. In one his cheek was against her hair. In another her lips brushed his ear. She looked up at him, her heart in her eyes. He looked down at her, brushed a hand through her hair.

"You might have been happy," her father allowed, "if you had had the time together to learn to love each other. But not, my Anny—" he touched her cheek, tucked a strand of her hair behind her ear "—when you are already in love with someone else."

She was in love with someone else. And she believed he loved her.

He would come to his senses, she told herself. He would see that they belonged together, that their lives were incomplete without her.

But if he did, she never heard about it.

Her father took her back to Mont Chamion and she spent a few days with him and her stepmother and her little half brothers. She thought he would come there, would sweep her off her feet, promise her undying love, ask her to marry him and live happily ever after.

That was what Prince Charming did, after all.

Pity she hadn't left a sandal behind, she thought grimly. Not that it would have done much good. Days passed.

Before a week was up she left Mont Chamion and went back to Cannes. Tante Isabelle had come home in the meantime, and she took one look at Anny and said, "My dear, you need a holiday and some rest."

Anny laughed. "I had a holiday," she said. "I just came back."

"Well, don't tell me where you went," Tante Isabelle said. "If it has made you this pale and miserable, I do not want to know."

Anny had left a message for Franck when she'd left Cannes after breaking her engagement. In it she'd told him he'd given her the courage to make a move, to take a risk. She was determined to smile and assure him it had been the right thing to do regardless of how miserable she felt.

But Franck wasn't there.

She felt a stab of panic at the sight of a complete stranger in Franck's bed until Sister Adelaide, the head nurse, reassured her. "He has gone to Paris. For surgery."

"Surgery?" Anny knew about the surgical option. Franck had mentioned it. It was experimental. A new technique that might relieve pressure if the nerves weren't dead. If it was successful and you worked like mad, exercised within an inch of your life, you might walk again. Might. Maybe. A little bit.

As far as she knew, he'd rejected the whole idea.

Sister Adelaide said, "He said you gave him the courage to do it."

Anny gaped. "Me?" Oh, yes, that was her, the poster child for taking risks.

"And Luke St. Angier," Sister Adelaide went on. "The actor. I forget his name. Very handsome."

"Demetrios Savas." Anny was proud of herself for being able to say his name as if her heart weren't breaking.

Sister Adelaide smiled. "*Oui*. Monsieur Savas. You know he came back several times during the festival?"

"Yes. They went sailing."

Sister beamed. "I think that was a big influence. And then the last day, before he left he came bringing Franck a whole folder of information about the surgery. He'd printed it out from articles he'd looked up online. He said it was important to be informed, but that was only a start. Ultimately you had to decide what mattered—what you were willing to risk. You had to ask yourself what you were afraid of—and decide if it was worth it.

Whatever Franck was afraid of, he'd made his decision.

"When is his surgery?"

"Next week."

"And then?"

Sister Adelaide smiled. "And then we will see. Franck will recover. He will exercise. He will work very very hard. If he walks, he will be very very happy. It is his dream."

Anny prayed that he would get his dream. She knew his fear and admired him for risking disappointment. It wasn't easy, she knew. And not all endings were happy. She knew that, too.

She didn't want for Franck the pain of hopes dashed, of dreams that never would come true.

After Lissa's death, Demetrios shut himself off from the world.

He was the grieving widower, after all, the tragic bereaved spouse who had just lost the most beloved person in his life.

It wasn't hard to act the role. It was easier, in fact, than being honest.

There was nothing to gain from being honest. No one really wanted to know the truth.

His parents and his siblings might have suspected that things weren't all they should be between him and Lissa. But he'd never told them. He hadn't wanted them to worry about him. And it was no one else's business.

Besides, after Lissa died, he had been grieving, just not for what everyone thought he was.

So he went off by himself. He spent six months at a beach house on the Oregon coast, running on the sand, swimming in the ocean, and trying to write out his pain and frustration. He'd grown fit and strong, and his pain and frustration had made a hell of a screenplay.

When it was done, he'd seen it as a way to get his life back.

So he'd taken it. He'd got financing, made his movie, found his place in the world again. He'd gone to Cannes telling himself he was whole again.

What a laugh.

He wasn't even close to whole. His life now was even more

of a fiction than his perfect marriage to Lissa had been—because he was lying to himself.

He had left his family in Santorini the day after Anny had left. He'd told them he had to get back to work. And he'd gone. He'd flown back to Hollywood, gone to script meetings, production meetings, design meetings, casting meetings. He'd pretended he was fine, that he could cope, that life would go on now just as it had after Lissa's death.

But he wasn't getting over Anny. He couldn't lie to himself about that.

He sat in the spacious opulent Southern California house he had shared with Lissa, staring at its multitude of walls and plate glass windows and felt a soul-wearying emptiness. In his mind's eye he saw the cramped quarters of the sailboat he'd shared with Anny and remembered laughter, happiness, joy.

He dived into his pool and swam countless meaningless laps. Inside he remembered the frustration that had driven him to dive into the roiling Mediterranean sea to try to get Anny out of his mind.

He lay in his wide solitary bed—a new one that he had never shared with Lissa—and remembered the two nights he'd spent making love with Anny.

He remembered her softness, her warmth, her smooth skin and shining hair, her hands that had learned him even as he had learned her. He remembered her wrapping herself around him, drawing him in, making the two of them whole together.

He would never be whole without Anny.

Never.

He padded from room to room, telling himself to stop thinking about the past, to focus on the future. But when he faced the truth he knew that the only future he wanted was with Anny.

Anny.

She'd taken a risk when she'd broken off her engagement with Gerard.

The boy Franck, Demetrios knew from a series of e-mails, had taken a risk by having the surgery.

They'd both credited him with giving them the courage.

"It's what you would do," Franck had written.

Was it? Demetrios wondered now. Or did he just talk a good fight?

Mont Chamion was a small country. But it was big enough to get lost in—if you wanted to—even if you were the crown princess.

Especially if you were a crown princess needing some time and space—a few days on her own—without her worried papa, her gentle stepmama, her rambunctious, inquisitive brothers.

Anny knew all the out-of-the-way rooms in the palace. She knew which bookcase to press to open the secret door to the turret. She knew how to find great-grandfather's folly in the woods and the best time to be alone in the summer house. But none of them would give her more than the respite of an hour or two.

Now that her brothers were older, there were fewer places she could go that they couldn't find her. They took great joy in it. And it had become something of a game in the last couple of years. A sort of royal hide-and-seek.

They'd played it often since she'd come home after her trip to Santorini. After Demetrios. Papa had wanted her here. She knew it even though he hadn't insisted. The boys had.

"You're gone too much," her middle brother, Raoul, had told her.

The youngest, four-year-old David, had climbed into her lap and said, "It's no fun without you, Anny."

And Alexandre, who, at nearly eight, was becoming aware of his responsibilities said, "Papa worries about you, Anny. You should stay here where we can take care of you."

And so she had stayed. For a while. To make them happy. To reassure her father. To spend time with her stepmother and her brothers. To feel loved because she was still raw from Demetrios's rejection.

But she'd been here nearly three weeks now. A long time. Too long. She should go back to Cannes again and get to work. But going back would mean facing every day remembering what had happened there. Remembering Demetrios.

As if she would ever forget.

She wouldn't. She knew that. But just as she and Papa had had to go on after her mother's death, she knew she had to go on now.

And so this morning she had asked her father for the key to the lake cabin.

"Are you sure, my Anny?" he asked. "There are memories there…."

"Good ones," Anny said firmly. "I am sure, Papa."

He had raised his brows silently and rolled his pen between the palms of his hands. "No one goes there now," he warned her. "It was our place. I never took Charlise and the boys. They have seen it, but the gardens are overgrown. It is old and dusty and run-down. Are you sure you will not be too lonely. Is it really a good idea?"

"Yes, it is. I'll clean it," Anny said. "Please, Papa. Just for a few days. I need some space. And," she added, " the boys won't find me there."

He smiled. But as he reached into his desk drawer and drew out the key, he said, "You hope."

The cabin was as old and dusty as he'd predicted. But to Anny it brought back wonderful memories. Some were sad. But she didn't regret them. And as she cleaned and scrubbed and swept and washed windows she felt herself settling down, coming to terms, putting things into perspective.

When her mother died, Papa had brought her here to remember. "We will look back," he had said. "We will remember. We will carry her with us as we go on."

She would do that now. Only this time she would remember Demetrios.

And then she would go on.

As night fell and the sky darkened, she went out onto the porch and, wrapped in a shawl in the cool mountain air, she sat down and stared up, watching as first one star and then another star winked into sight.

Wishing stars, Mama had called them.

Conversation starters, she thought with an ache in her throat, remembering the nights with Demetrios.

She started to shove the thought away, to think about the future. But then she stopped. She let the memories come. She had come here to remember. She didn't have to go on—not just yet.

She looked up at the stars and she wished.

She wished for Demetrios to find happiness. She wished he would know love. She wished that someday he would realize love wasn't only painful, that it could bring joy.

She wished it would bring her a little joy. Someday. Somehow.

Mostly she wished she would stop crying. She swallowed hard and scrubbed at her eyes.

And then she heard the footsteps. Light. Hesitant. Unsure of their way.

Oh, Papa! she thought despairingly, knowing what he had done. He'd worried about her being here by herself. He'd given the boys hints. Maybe not David, but Alexandre and Raoul were old enough that he would let them follow these paths. He knew she wouldn't turn them away.

She straightened and cleared her throat. "I hear you," she said. "You can stop sneaking around."

"Anny? Thank God."

She almost fell off the porch. Then, tripping over the shawl, she stumbled to her feet. "*Demetrios*?"

She stared in amazement into the darkness, wondering if she were hallucinating, as a tall lean man picked his way up the narrow overgrown path, then stopped at the foot of the steps and looked up at her.

She couldn't read his expression. From his stance he looked wary, uncertain. Pretty much the way she felt, Anny thought. Her knees were shaking. She clutched the porch rail to keep herself upright.

"What are you doing here?"

"Right now? Thanking God I found you," he said with a shaky laugh. "I almost don't believe it."

"Neither do I," Anny said, which had to be the understatement of the year. She wanted simply to stare at him, to drink in the sight of him—what little she could actually see in the darkness.

She wanted to pinch herself to be sure she wasn't dreaming. She didn't even know why he was here.

Finally she remembered her manners. "Would you like to come in?" she said politely. "I can make some coffee. I have some biscuits."

He made a sound that was half sob, half laugh. "Oh God, Anny, I've missed you. Yes," he said coming up the steps, so close now she could touch him. "I'd like to come in. I'd like coffee. I'd like biscuits. I love you."

She stared at him, stunned, disbelieving. He was right in front of her, his shirt brushing against her sweater, his breath warm against her face. Real. And saying the words earnestly, not grudgingly. She opened her mouth and closed it again.

He didn't move away. He touched her cheek, tipped her face so that she looked straight into his eyes. The only light she had to see them by was starlight. It was enough. "I mean it," he said urgently. "I love you, Anny. I have since—hell, I don't know when! But it isn't going away. I'm glad it isn't going away," he said fiercely. "You know I love you. You told me I did," he said, sounding a little desperate at her silence.

Anny nodded numbly. "Yes, but—"

"But I didn't want to hear it." He shook his head. "And I still don't know what to do about it. I have so little to offer you. I failed Lissa—"

She couldn't stay silent now. "You *didn't* fail Lissa!"

"I didn't help her. I couldn't reach her. I didn't even really know her."

"You knew me. You reached me. You gave me strength and courage and hope. And love," she told him. And she felt her throat tighten and feared she would start crying again, so she took his hand. "Come in."

She led him into the cabin and switched on the light, and felt her heart kick over at the sight of him.

He wore a long-sleeved, open-neck denim shirt, a rough canvas jacket and a pair of clean but faded jeans. He was clean-shaven now, and his thick dark hair had been neatly trimmed. He was every bit as gorgeous as she remembered. As far as she was concerned, there was no man on earth with a stronger, more masculine, yet more beautiful face.

But beautiful as they always were, his eyes were different tonight. On the boat they had watched her, but had always held her at a distance. Even when they'd made love and they'd warmed with desire and clouded with passion, they'd still held her off.

Tonight they invited her in.

And Anny didn't need any more explanation than that. She trusted his love. She trusted his being here. She framed his face with her hands and raised herself on her toes to touch her lips to his.

In an instant his arms wrapped around her. He crushed her against him, burying his face in her hair. She felt a tremor run through him, and she knew her own heart hammered with the joy of the hallelujah chorus in her chest.

"I love you," he said again. His words teased the tendrils of her hair, touched her ears. And her heart.

"I love you, too," she vowed.

He kissed her cheek, her temple, her hair, then down her jawline to her mouth. His tongue parted her lips, tasted her, and she tasted him in return. Her arms slid up to go around his neck. He wrapped her close, drew her against him, and she felt how well they fit—as if they belonged together. Because they did. He deepened the kiss. His fingers traced the line down her spine, cupped her buttocks and held her against him, let her feel the need that matched her own.

Then she pulled back. "Are you sure you want coffee and biscuits?"

He laughed. "I'd rather have you."

She took his hand to draw him toward the bedroom. "That can be arranged."

But he didn't move. "Not just tonight," he said, his hooded eyes dark. "Always." He ran his tongue over his lips. "I didn't know the protocol," he said. "But I asked your father if he'd agree to my asking you to marry me."

Anny's eyes widened. "You talked to my father?"

He nodded. "You weren't in Cannes. You weren't in Berkeley." At her surprise, he added, "Tante Isabelle said she didn't know where you were. You might be in Berkeley defending your dissertation."

"Not yet," Anny said, smiling, knowing Tante Isabelle well enough to know she'd been determined to make the man who'd broken her goddaughter's heart prove his mettle before he found her.

"So I discovered," Demetrios said. "So I went to the palace. Without an appointment. That's apparently not done."

But he'd done it. "Papa would have wanted to talk to you."

"Oh, yeah, he did. Gave me an earful. Wouldn't tell me where you were."

"And then relented when he saw you meant it?"

Demetrios shook his head. "No. He said I could damned well find you myself if I loved you." He squared his shoulders. "So I did."

She stared. "No one but Papa knew where I went."

"But your brothers at least knew you were in Mont Chamion. And your father said you didn't want distractions. That you didn't need to be bothered. So I knew where you'd gone."

She stared. "You did?"

"You told me about this place. Your refuge by the lake where you wished on the stars. Where you'd gone after your mother died. I guess I didn't know for sure," he admitted. "I hoped. So I asked your father for directions to the lake house. And that was when, I think, he realized you'd trusted me with something you didn't talk about to everyone. There was a faint crack in the royal facade."

She smiled. "Yes. We don't talk about the cabin to anyone."

"So he gave me the directions—along with an introduction to his sword collection and word about what a good fencer he is." Demetrios's mouth twisted wryly. "I am allowed to ask you to marry me. He said it was up to you—but if you said yes, I'd better never hurt you again."

Anny laughed. Her heart was near to bursting. "You won't." She knew that for a fact. If he'd faced his demons and come looking for her, she had nothing at all to fear. "So are…you asking me?"

"Will you marry me, Anny?" He didn't stop there. "You are everything I've ever wanted—a woman to share with, to talk with, to joke with, to sail with, to ride out a storm with." He swallowed. "To have a family with."

It was her turn to kiss him then. To run her fingers lightly over his scalp, to stroke his now short hair and nuzzle his smooth-shaven cheek and inhale—and cherish anew—the scent of him.

"You are everything I ever wanted, too," she told him. "Not just the man on the poster. The man I met in Cannes. The man I sailed with. The man I made love with—fell in love with. Yes, I'll marry you, Demetrios. And have a family with you," she whispered. "Yes. Oh yes, please."

Royal weddings took an inordinate amount of time to arrange. If, Charlise told her stepdaughter, you wanted to do them right.

"By right, I mean, with all proper pomp and circumstance, protocol and rigamarole." She paused. "But if what you want is the right man and the right woman and the right people there to celebrate with you, I think we can do it in six months."

Anny goggled. "Six months?"

"A year would be better. Or two."

Demetrios wasn't going to wait a year. Certainly not two. Six months would be a strain, Anny knew. For both of them. But they'd discussed it and she knew he was willing to deal with her royal obligations.

"It's who you are," he'd said. "I love you."

Now that he was saying it, he said it often. She never tired of hearing it. They both said it every night.

He was philosophical about the six months. "They can't expect me to wait on the same continent that long," he'd said. "I'll go to Mexico and work on my film."

But he'd called her every night. They'd talked. They'd laughed. They'd argued about how many children they'd have and what they'd name them. And every other week either she'd flown out to him or he'd come to Mont Chamion to spend a few days with her.

Even so, they were the longest six months of Anny's life. She had a thousand decisions to make, but as she told Charlise, "It's not really important. I've made the only decision that matters."

"You have," Charlise agreed. And so did Papa.

He had welcomed Demetrios into the family. Besides his introduction to the sword collection, Demetrios had been given a long lecture about his responsibilities to his new bride. But at the end, he'd shaken Demetrios's hand and wrapped him in a warm embrace.

"You love her. I can see that. And I know she loves you. The kingdom is of far less importance than my daughter's happiness. She will be your wife and you will love each other," he told Demetrios. "That's what matters. The rest—we will work it out."

Now, as she waited with her father to walk down the aisle on the morning of their wedding, Anny lifted her veil and leaned up to kiss him. "I love you, Papa. Thank you so much for being my father. For trusting me."

"You will smear your lipstick," he chided her, even as he kissed her cheek and brushed a tear from his eye. "Of course I trust you. How could I not? You are my daughter, the light of my life."

She would have cried then, but she couldn't. Not yet. No one wanted to watch her walk down the aisle with tears streaming down her face.

Just then the introductory organ music paused dramatically— and plunged into the formal wedding march.

Her father touched her hand. "It is time."

Demetrios's sister, Tallie, his sister-in-law, Martha, and Martha's sister, Cristina, and dear Tante Isabelle were her bridesmaids.

One by one they preceded her down the aisle.

And then it was her turn. Papa's fingers squeezed hers, and then together, slowly, they made their way down the aisle.

The church was filled to the rafters with people come to cheer on Mont Chamion's only princess and her handsome, clearly besotted groom.

For the past six months all the tabloids had been writing about the upcoming royal wedding. They'd written endlessly about Anny and revisited over and over the charmed life Demetrios Savas had lived. They wrote about his talent, his Hollywood career, his perfect short-lived first marriage, how he had mourned as a recluse the death of his first beloved wife. But now, they wrote, while it was tragic, it was a codicil to his nearly perfect life.

Demetrios never contradicted it. He said how delighted he was, how Anny's love made him the happiest man on earth. He never alluded to the past except when asked, and then as always, he was honorable. He was kind.

Because that's the sort of man he was, Anny knew. Only she knew the truth. She knew the man. She loved him more than life itself.

And as she walked down the aisle now, she could see him waiting, and in a row beside him, his brothers: Yiannis on the end, bemused and tapping his foot nervously, George, next to him, lean and watchful and seriously intent. Then Theo, tall and dark and smiling broadly.

And between Theo and Demetrios was the best man.

Anny stared, not quite able to believe her eyes, at a younger man, not as tall as the Savas brothers, dark-haired and very thin, grinning widely and standing tall, though he still leaned on two metal hand canes.

"Franck." Her step faltered. The tears began to fall.

Her father gave her a kiss and gave her hand to Demetrios. "Love her," he exhorted.

"I do," Demetrios vowed. "I always will."

And then, although it certainly wasn't protocol, he tipped the veil aside to peer in at her. "I thought you'd be crying." His expression was tender, his eyes were smiling as he shared her joy at Franck's presence, at his progress. At his dream come true.

"I can't believe he's here."

"He is. It was his goal as soon as I asked him," Demetrios told her. "But we'd better get this show on the road. He doesn't stand up for long."

The priest cleared his throat. "If you please."

Demetrios grinned and dropped her veil. He straightened and attempted to look serious. Anny squeezed his hand. He squeezed back.

"Dearly beloved," the priest intoned.

And Anny, looking around, knew how true that was. Everyone here—all their family, all their friends gathered to celebrate their wedding with them—was dear and beloved. All of them gave joy and meaning to her life.

But no one was more dear or beloved, no one gave her more joy or meaning than Demetrios.

Theo lent them the sailboat for their honeymoon.

They had to wait six weeks to take it because Demetrios had filming to finish. But Anny was philosophical.

"I'll get to watch you work," she said happily. "And," she added, "you can't work all the time."

No, he hadn't worked all the time. But he was looking forward to some time alone with Anny. Just the two of them. Back on the boat. Together.

"Don't wreck it while you're busy doing other things," Theo added gruffly.

"What other things?" Demetrios said with all the innocence he could muster.

Theo cuffed his shoulder and rolled his eyes, then he fixed Anny with a hard look. "He's got my boat to sail. Keep him in line," he said to Anny.

Anny laughed. "Not likely." And Demetrios grinned, too. She knew him all too well.

"Go away," he said to his brother now. "We'll be fine. Your boat will be fine. Stop bothering us."

Theo grinned. He made a few more adjustments. He made a few more comments. Mostly to annoy because that's what brothers did. But finally he left.

And so at last did they, Demetrios raising the sail as Anny steered her out away from Santorini's small harbor. They were sailing her to Cannes.

"The same, but different," Anny had said when he'd suggested it. Because they wouldn't be fighting their desire this time. They'd be spending their days sailing and their nights in each other's arms.

"Better," Demetrios vowed.

"Maybe," he said as he carried her over the threshold of their cabin that night, after a beautiful day of light winds and easy sailing, "we can get to work on those kids whose names we argue about."

He dropped her lightly on the bunk and dropped down to lie beside her, to undress her, to kiss her, to love her, to cherish her.

"I don't think so." Anny shook her head.

He stopped, stared at her.

She grinned and slid her arms around him, pulling him on top of her, wrapping him in her embrace. "We already have."

He stared, felt his heart kick over. "Anny?" He pulled back to look at her, to see if she was joking.

She smiled and gave a little wiggle beneath him. "It's true, Demetrios. In about seven and a half months Zorathustra will be here."

Demetrios stared. And then he grinned and kissed her. "You mean, Melchisedeck," he corrected.

Anny laughed. "Zorathustra."

"Melchisedeck."

Anny kissed him, laughing against his mouth. "Maybe I'll have twins."

Demetrios laughed, too, and rolled her in his arms. "Fine with me, princess." Everything was fine with him. Life was beautiful. Anny was beautiful. And, dear God, he loved her. "Maybe you will."

Coming Next Month

in Harlequin Presents® EXTRA. Available September 14, 2010.

Coming Next Month

in Harlequin Presents®. Available September 28, 2010.

LARGER-PRINT BOOKS!

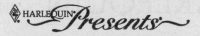

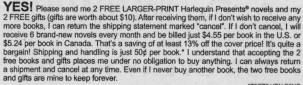

GET 2 FREE LARGER-PRINT NOVELS PLUS 2 FREE GIFTS!

YES! Please send me 2 FREE LARGER-PRINT Harlequin Presents® novels and my 2 FREE gifts (gifts are worth about $10). After receiving them, if I don't wish to receive any more books, I can return the shipping statement marked "cancel." If I don't cancel, I will receive 6 brand-new novels every month and be billed just $4.55 per book in the U.S. or $5.24 per book in Canada. That's a saving of at least 13% off the cover price! It's quite a bargain! Shipping and handling is just 50¢ per book.* I understand that accepting the 2 free books and gifts places me under no obligation to buy anything. I can always return a shipment and cancel at any time. Even if I never buy another book, the two free books and gifts are mine to keep forever.

176/376 HDN E5NG

Name	(PLEASE PRINT)	
Address		Apt. #
City	State/Prov.	Zip/Postal Code

Signature (if under 18, a parent or guardian must sign)

Mail to the **Harlequin Reader Service:**
IN U.S.A.: P.O. Box 1867, Buffalo, NY 14240-1867
IN CANADA: P.O. Box 609, Fort Erie, Ontario L2A 5X3

Not valid for current subscribers to Harlequin Presents Larger-Print books.

**Are you a subscriber to Harlequin Presents books and want to receive the larger-print edition?
Call 1-800-873-8635 today!**

* Terms and prices subject to change without notice. Prices do not include applicable taxes. Sales tax applicable in N.Y. Canadian residents will be charged applicable provincial taxes and GST. Offer not valid in Quebec. This offer is limited to one order per household. All orders subject to approval. Credit or debit balances in a customer's account(s) may be offset by any other outstanding balance owed by or to the customer. Please allow 4 to 6 weeks for delivery. Offer available while quantities last.

Your Privacy: Harlequin Books is committed to protecting your privacy. Our Privacy Policy is available online at www.eHarlequin.com or upon request from the Reader Service. From time to time we make our lists of customers available to reputable third parties who may have a product or service of interest to you. If you would prefer we not share your name and address, please check here. ☐

Help us get it right—We strive for accurate, respectful and relevant communications. To clarify or modify your communication preferences, visit us at www.ReaderService.com/consumerchoice.

HPLP10R

HARLEQUIN®

A *Romance*

FOR EVERY MOOD™

Spotlight on

Inspirational

Wholesome romances
that touch the heart and soul.

See the next page
to enjoy a sneak peek from
the Love Inspired® inspirational series.

*See below for a sneak peek at
our inspirational line, Love Inspired®.
Introducing HIS HOLIDAY BRIDE
by bestselling author Jillian Hart*

Autumn Granger gave her horse rein to slide toward the town's new sheriff.

"Hey, there." The man in a brand-new Stetson, black T-shirt, jeans and riding boots held up a hand in greeting. He stepped away from his four-wheel drive with "Sheriff" in black on the doors and waded through the grasses. "I'm new around here."

"I'm Autumn Granger."

"Nice to meet you, Miss Granger. I'm Ford Sherman, from Chicago." He knuckled back his hat, revealing the most handsome face she'd ever seen. Big blue eyes contrasted with his sun-tanned complexion.

"I'm guessing you haven't seen much open land. Out here, you've got to keep an eye on cows or they're going to tear your vehicle apart."

"What?" He whipped around. Sure enough, mammoth black-and-white creatures had started to gnaw on his four-wheel drive. They clustered like a mob, mouths and tongues and teeth bent on destruction. One cow tried to pry the wiper off the windshield, another chewed on the side mirror. Several leaned through the open window, licking the seats.

"Move along, little dogie." He didn't know the first thing about cattle.

The entire herd swiveled their heads to study him curiously. Not a single hoof shifted. The animals soon returned to chewing, licking, digging through his possessions.

Autumn laughed, a warm and wonderful sound. "Thanks,

I needed that." She then pulled a bag from behind her saddle and waved it at the cows. "Look what I have, guys. Cookies."

Cows swung in her direction, and dozens of liquid brown eyes brightened with cookie hopes. As she circled the car, the cattle bounded after her. The earth shook with the force of their powerful hooves.

"Next time, you're on your own, city boy." She tipped her hat. The cowgirl stayed on his mind, the sweetest thing he had ever seen.

*Will Ford be able to stick it out in the country
to find out more about Autumn?
Find out in HIS HOLIDAY BRIDE
by bestselling author Jillian Hart,
available in October 2010
only from Love Inspired®.*

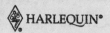